JOSIAH WHITBY

JOSIAH WHITBY

a novel by
Eli Alexander

Ambassador International
Greenville, South Carolina & Belfast, Northern Ireland
www.ambassador-international.com

Josiah Whitby
a novel by Eli Alexander

© 2011 by Eli Alexander
All rights reserved

Printed in the United States of America

ISBN: 9781935507710

Cover & Page Design by David Siglin

AMBASSADOR INTERNATIONAL
Emerald House
427 Wade Hampton Blvd.
Greenville, SC 29609, USA
www.ambassador-international.com

AMBASSADOR BOOKS
The Mount
2 Woodstock Link
Belfast, BT6 8DD, Northern Ireland, UK
www.ambassador-international.com

The colophon is a trademark of Ambassador

DEDICATED

to Kelley, my wife

Erin, Chloe, & Sophie, my daughters

Special thanks to my grandparents for inspiration:

J.K. & Leona East

James & Eleanor Ledbetter

AN OFFICIAL PRINTING
OF THE JOURNAL OF
JOSIAH WHITBY

EPIPHANY

MAY 1, 1858
BAPTIST SEMINARY OF THE SOUTH—RICHMOND, VA

TODAY, I BEGIN THIS journal as I feel I have experienced an epiphany. A moment in my life that may eternally change its direction. A moment when you realize who you really are or who you really should be. I am Josiah Whitby. Having spent the last 5 years studying to be a minister, I have experienced more than a few changes. I feel I was called to serve others early in life. It is my mission, my duty.

I was raised in Charleston, South Carolina, Johns Island to be specific. I am the son of a cotton farmer. My father is a rather stoic man. Stern but loving. Simple yet wise. My mother is a kind and gentle woman who always made me feel loved. Although we were far from wealthy, farming only 40 acres, my father owned 4 slaves. This was the norm in the South. Miss Mamie, an elderly African woman, helped raise me. I can honestly say I loved her. She seemed to care for me, but whether out of love or necessity, I am not sure.

The subject of slavery is at the center of my revelation. Pastor Simon, an elderly instructor at the Seminary, was lecturing on Jesus' Commandments. After a lengthy oration, he finished with what is considered the most important of all the commandments: "Love thy neighbor as thyself," or more simply put "Love one another." Somehow the words came out of my mouth, "Is the African our neighbor? Should the Christian love the African as well?" As you can imagine, there was a gasp in the classroom followed by an uncomfortable silence. You see, all of those who studied alongside me were raised in the Southern states. Not all owned slaves, but they accepted the practice as normal. The question of whether slavery was right or wrong was not discussed. Does one debate the existence of the wind? Slavery was the wind. A mysterious force that could move and shape, but was too big, too engrained to contemplate. Ironically enough, one of my favorite Biblical passages is "Sow the wind, and reap the whirlwind."

After the prolonged silence, the elderly Pastor Simon removed his spectacles and said, "There are two answers to your question. One practical and one Biblical. Today, practicality is the order of things. Eventually, a greater force may prevail. Just because the sun rises every day does not mean we should not ask why does the sun rise or what would happen if the sun fails to rise. If I am to be honest, Jesus died for all people. That is the truth."

Pastor Simon paused. It was clear that he had pondered this same question. It was also clear that he understood the order of things in today's Southern society. He went on, "You all will go back to your hometowns in a few weeks and you will become the leaders of local churches. You must also consider the realities you will face. Preaching is never a popularity contest, but staying employed sometimes is."

Pastor Simon was one of my mentors at Seminary. He knew the Bible, he understood the world, and he could relate to the common man. I strived to be more like him. His answers to these difficult questions took into account the realities we all must face.

At that point I was confused. I knew that something had changed in me but I was not sure what. I believed that I might return to my beloved Charleston and preach to the hearts of man and subtly try to improve the treatment of the slaves. Looking back, my cause was greater and more challenging than I ever imagined. It was clear that I was no longer in charge of my life, but a much greater force was pulling me straight into the whirlwind.

During that last week of seminary, I committed to researching the Bible's depiction of slavery. Was it inherently wrong for one man to own another man, as was the practice in the South? For that matter, was it wrong to employ someone in deplorable conditions and pay them a wage that was negligible, as was the practice in Northern factories? Was it wrong to prevent a group of people from living in your state, as was the norm in many other areas? A law in and of itself is rarely inhumane. Human action based upon these laws creates the immorality. Were these practices wrong in and of themselves or was the inhumanity, the lack of love, the actual sin?

I concluded that the inhumane treatment of another human was inconsistent with God's Word. Under any title or circumstance, that was wrong. I really did not need to dig any further than the passage "Love one another."

So there I was pondering my very existence, my upbringing, the soul of the Southern identity. It was clear that the Southern culture and ideals were not all invalid. The family-centered life, hard work, Sunday mornings at church, Sunday afternoons spent with family. Woven throughout was the influence of the Africans. The food, the nurturing of the children, the tireless laboring, and most of all the unbreakable spirit. They were the water of the Southern existence. Water does not define a man, but it does sustain him. It is essential to his being.

The South and Charleston in particular had a very high African population. In many areas, the number of persons of color far surpassed the white Europeans. This led to an interesting yet volatile dynamic. There was the constant fear that the slaves may organize and revolt. Such an occurrence, en masse, would be almost impossible to quell.

Charleston also went through periods when free slaves owned property and were welcomed into the aristocracy of Charleston society. They ran many of the fine restaurants and hotels. Periodically, a slave conspiracy would be uncovered and the free slaves would be forced to flee Charleston. The free people of color were almost never involved in such conspiracies, but a mob mentality often takes over during times such as these. Rational thought is left behind.

There was also a large group of slaves that were permitted by their masters to work for pay as skilled craftsmen. These laborers often competed with poor whites for jobs. This furthered the racial tension even among the lower economic class in the South.

After significant thought and research, my deep wonderings were satisfied. I concluded that slavery was evil. This was an easy deduction, just as one could say stealing or murder was wrong. But what to do with my new-found knowledge was unclear. I decided to return home as planned and take up a position alongside my childhood minister, Pastor Isaiah Phillips. He had been the leader of Johns Island Church for 30 years and was revered among the 100-plus members of the congregation. I would be stepping back into my old world with my new values.

JOURNEY

THE JOURNEY BACK TO Charleston from Richmond would take a week or more. Luckily, I was able to purchase a horse and wagon to make the trip. Many of my classmates were forced to walk. Others had the means to take the new trains that were beginning to cross the southland. This time of year it begins to get quite warm and the trip would surely be an arduous one. Although it added to my discomfort, I decided to wear my new pastor collar and hat given to each graduate by the school. I was proud of my accomplishments, perhaps more than one should be.

On the third day, I crossed into North Carolina. I felt a sense of calm having entered the state that bordered my own. Our Sister to the North, as we often referred to her. This calm was soon shattered by one of my first moral challenges.

The hum of the gentle breeze was interrupted by a man, an African man, bloody and panting as if he were running from a pack of wild animals. He crossed the road and collapsed saying, "Please don't let them kill me, Lord, please don't." Again, as I had done in Pastor Simon's class, I acted without thought.

More likely I acted with a higher level of consciousness. I picked the man up and put him under my bags in the back of the wagon. I told him clearly if he even breathed too loud, we would both be hanged. The man managed to calm himself in a few seconds. He did not know if I would really help him, but he knew the alternative was far worse.

A short while later several men approached on horses inquiring about a lost slave. My heart raced. Those who helped escaped slaves usually were treated no better than the escapees. Hanging, beating, and whipping were just the beginning of the reward. In addition, I was a man of God. Was it all right to lie? Can I commit one sin to prevent another? If I was caught helping a slave escape, I may never preach in the South again. It is amazing how many thoughts one can concoct while staring at the face of fear.

One man asked, "Pastor, have you seen an escaped savage?"

Fortunately, I could answer this question with complete honesty. "The only person I have seen was one of your neighbors but I will surely be on the lookout for any savages."

The other man stated, "Thank you kindly, Pastor, and will you surely pray that we find our property?"

I replied, "I will surely pray for you sir, I surely will."

A few miles down the road, I found a small grove of trees beside a stream. I pulled off to the side and carried the African man to a sheltered area. After I gave him some water and some food that I had packed for my trip, he asked, "Why would you do that? Why would you help a man like me?"

"I don't know," I replied. "Sometimes people do the right thing even when everyone else thinks it is wrong."

I wrapped some food in a small piece of cloth and sent him on his way. "Good luck, neighbor."

I did not even get the man's name that I helped. As funny as it sounds, I felt wrong for calling him a man. That shows you how engrained the slave culture was. Of course he was a man. Same as me. A man with hopes, dreams, a past, a future. No more or no less valuable than anyone else.

I cannot fully explain what happened that day. It was as if someone else controlled me. I was a puppet. I even felt some guilt, but why?

The next few days were somewhat uneventful. I proceeded through North Carolina. Roanoke Rapids, Rocky Mount, and on through Smithfield. I stayed at some inns along the way as well as spending time with old family friends. It is funny how few slaves you see in the majority of the South. To hear the Northern folk tell it, we all have 100 slaves and beat them twice a day. There are clearly areas where that occurs, but on a good day in the country, the world seems sane.

I was very much looking forward to arriving in Horry County in South Carolina. That was the home of my mother's parents, Mr. & Mrs. J. K. East. Grandma and Grandpa, as I called them, had lived there for years and I would spend summers at their home. Grandpa was also a minister at Horry Baptist Church, one of the largest Baptist churches in South Carolina. My grandparents were another one of the factors that contributed to my joining the ministry. They always displayed such a sense of happiness and peace in their day-to-day activities. I do not ever remember Grandpa preaching to me about Jesus. I just remember wanting to learn more about the source of his contentment. In my short experience in life, I have learned that fear is not nearly as great a motivator as love is.

One other thing about Grandpa was that he regularly preached to the African slaves. He had convinced the local plantation owners that a Christian slave would be more disciplined and work harder.

A more earthly and selfish benefit to seeing my grandparents was getting to eat Grandma's cooking. They always had a garden full of corn, tomatoes, beans, watermelons, and whatever else they could find to plant. It is funny how some of your best memories are the simple ones and they usually involve good food.

Upon arrival at my grandparents' home, I was greeted warmly with a hug and a kiss. I believe I saw a tear in the eyes of both of them as they saw me in my minister collar. The biggest validation one can experience is to know that you have encouraged people to help others. I believe that is what they were feeling.

Grandpa took me on a tour of his garden as well as the new additions to the church adjacent to their home. When I picture myself in 40 years, I want to be doing the same thing with my grandchildren.

As I washed up for dinner that night, it all came back to me. My comments in Pastor Simon's class, my revelation, helping the slave. I felt that I had to ask my grandfather his opinion. I could not tell him everything because that would make him an accessory to my crime. As we sat down to a dinner of chicken and dumplings, turnip casserole, sweet potatoes, beans, and sweet tea, I began to ask my grandfather as well as my grandmother some questions. I was interested in both of their responses. My grandma was a very wise woman and a key advisor to my grandpa.

"I have been studying the Bible a lot over the past 5 years," I stated, "and I keep getting stuck on this one point. Jesus said the greatest commandment is to love your neighbor as yourself. Everyone seems to agree on that. But my question is who is my neighbor? Is it those who live around me? Is it the South? Is it everyone on earth? Is it only white folks?"

My Grandpa paused for a second and said, "Son, the answer is simple. Jesus said, 'Love one another.' He did not make any exclusions. Your grandma and I do not own slaves for that very reason. Now, that being said, does that mean I should be preaching the abolition of slavery in my church? That is a more challenging question. I would surely be imprisoned or hanged. A pro-slavery preacher would then replace me. What good would that serve? I hope I live to see the end of slavery and I will try to do my small part to help. Remember this, my grandson—a dead preacher only fills a church once, and that is on the day of his funeral."

My grandma then added, "All of these years that we have been preaching to the Africans, it was out of love and obligation. We had to tell the landowners it was for their benefit, but that was not it at all. It was the right thing to do. Previously you have inquired about our happiness and contentment. One is most content when he or she is doing good in this world. We must obey man's laws whenever possible, but we must obey God's laws all the time."

As is the pattern in my life at this time, the more I learn, the more uncertain I seem to be. I stayed another few days with Grandpa and Grandma before heading down the road toward Charleston. Being with them was peaceful. It always seemed like a haven from reality.

HOME

ON THE OUTSKIRTS OF the Charleston area, I began to see familiar sites. The tall Palmetto trees, muscadine vines, and jasmine all lined the country roads. A few magnolia trees were in bloom. That smell, the sweet citrus smell of a magnolia, was one of my favorites. These trees were evergreen and had a lot of low branches. As a kid, my friends and me would climb up to the top and survey the land and the marsh. It felt like you could see the whole world from there, at least our whole world. That was one of the problems with the South and the North. Neither believed the world extended beyond their sight.

On this return trip, I would bypass Charleston, going just west of the city. Johns Island is just to the southwest of downtown Charleston, only a few hours' carriage ride from our home. Several large plantations as well as many small family farms dominated the island. The land was very fertile, having been occupied and farmed by ancient Kiawah Indians in days gone by.

Upon entering the gates to my family's farm, I stopped. Unbelievably, I was very nervous. I felt somewhat like a stranger.

Not only was I much older than the last time I was home two years ago, I was also in a different frame of mind. The Josiah that left here would never come back. I tried to suppress all of those feelings for the time being. I just wanted to be home. To be myself. To relax. I would sort out everything else in a few days.

The first person I saw as I approached the house was Miss Mamie, the elderly African woman who helped to take care of me when I was young. Upon seeing me, she dropped to her knees and cried, "My baby come home, my baby come home." This was real, pure emotion. Many if not most slaves deplored their masters; our relationship with Mamie and Jackson was different. Clearly we had complete control over their lives, but it was more like a business relationship. Don't get me wrong, it was still a degrading arrangement for one man to own another, but the difference was we treated them as humans.

Although communication among slaves at different households was strictly forbidden, there was always some way in which they stayed in touch with one another. The fear always was that they would plan a revolt. A well-organized revolt involving all of them. This would be almost impossible to quell. Their communication was how they knew the condition and treatment of their family members and friends that were sold to other owners. I must say the thought of splitting a family was unconscionable to me. That was one practice that I was opposed to even before my great awakening.

After I gave Mamie a hug, she said, "You a man of the Lord now. Do good. Do right." Many of the slaves in the South were

Christians. The belief was that a Christian slave might be easier to manage.

Jackson, Miss Mamie's husband and the foreman of our farm, was working in the field. He also came in to greet me. He said, "You ought be mighty proud of yourself, Master Josiah. We is too." I thanked him for his comments and he promptly returned to the fields. It was ironic that I saw both Miss Mamie and Jackson before I saw my own parents. This probably was more coincidence than symbolism, but everything seemed to have a meaning now.

At the house, both of my parents rushed to meet my carriage. They were both clearly glad to see me. My father even seemed to have a look of pride on his face. He was a loving man, but rarely showed emotions. The next few hours were spent catching up on the events of the past year. My mother and I had exchanged several letters during my training, but it is hard to keep up to date when it takes weeks or months to receive a letter.

That night, my father asked Mamie and Jackson to join us inside the house for a dinner celebrating my return. This was highly unusual in Southern society. But it seemed appropriate because the person I was and the person I was becoming was shaped by both sides of that table. Although we had interacted for years with our slaves, it was rare to sit and eat with them. It was a little awkward watching all of us sit together and interact as though we were equals. In Southern society a meal always seems to bring people together. My great grandmother used to say that we could solve all of the world's ills over a Sunday dinner. I realized that the more you treat someone as an equal, the more they start to act like one.

The next day I was to meet with Pastor Phillips at my home church. It was my hope that Johns Island Church and Pastor Phillips would serve as my mentors for several years. During this time, I would be able to hone my skills, learn to manage the finances of the church, and also learn to deal with the political realities within institutions such as this. My ultimate goal was to start my own church.

I turned in for the night. It was good to be back in my own bed, my own room. It felt good. Surprisingly, I slept well. I did awake at first light, but that was usual both while I was in school as well as here on the farm. If the roosters didn't wake you then my father would. After a nice breakfast, I headed out to the church. I went alone. Again, I was trying to establish myself as an adult. I was now 20 years old. It was time that I made my way.

The church was only about 1 mile away from our home. It took about 30 minutes to get there. As you approach the church, the old cemetery is the first thing you see. I never knew a lot about who was buried there except for a few neighbors. Most of my kin, including my sister, were buried on family property.

As I reached the church, I tied up the team to the hitching post and proceeded to the door of the church. Pastor Phillips's house was adjacent to the church, but I figured he would be waiting on me inside the church. As I entered the empty church, I heard a thunderous voice: "Well, well, our junior pastor has arrived and only 10 minutes late. I suppose the congregation will be able to sleep in on Sunday morning."

I was a little nervous and a little embarrassed, but you have to know Pastor Phillips. He has a flair for the dramatic. He loves to speak loudly in his quintessential "Chaaarleston" accent. He went on, "Welcome son. I know you are going to work out just fine here. With some guidance from me and some blessings from the Lord, who knows, I may let you preach a sermon in a year or two."

I had already assumed that I would probably be an errand boy for the Pastor. I would clean up the church, keep the books, buy supplies, and do any other odd jobs that Pastor Phillips needed. This is somewhat common. While I stepped out of Seminary knowing a lot about Jesus, I needed to learn how to manage a church.

Pastor Phillips began by giving me a tour of the church and its grounds. It was almost as though he forgot that I had attended services there each Sunday for my first 15 years. It was a great experience, though. I saw a different side to the Pastor. He had great pride and satisfaction in the church he had helped to develop. He would say things like, "See that pew over there, Edward Fillmore and his boys gave us that." He would go on, "These candles were made for us by Elvira Munstead." The reality was that most of these items were made by the slaves of those people. But it was customary to credit the slave owner for the slave's efforts. This was another example of pride propping up the perversion.

As we walked outside, I asked the Pastor about the cemetery. "Who all is buried here? All of our kin is buried back home."

The Pastor paused and seemed a bit retrospective. "Son," he said, "this church was first established before the Revolutionary War. Many of the heroes of Cowpens, Kings Mountain, and those that fought with Francis Marion are buried here. The heroes who defended our beloved city of Charleston from the occupying British forces are laid here as well. There are records in the basement of the church. True heroes helped establish and maintain this church since its inception. I hope you realize the expectations that God has for you." Pastor Phillips paused and looked out over the salt marsh that was adjacent to the property.

He then continued, "That mausoleum over there was built as a memorial to the Revolutionary War heroes. Construction was begun right before the War. Ain't nobody buried in it though. It's empty. My mentor, Pastor Jeremiah, said that they opened it once. I never saw the need. I know the Lord will protect me if I was to encounter some evil sprits, but the good Lord also gave me the good sense not to go lookin' for them too."

In these times, spirits were much talked about. Partially because of the influence of the African culture and partially because we heard and saw a lot of strange things on this island.

I spent the rest of the day being shown the inner workings of our church. You do not think about all of the efforts that go into a Sunday morning service until you have someone tell you all about it. I was also shown the basement of the church, which served as a storage area as well as a small workspace for Pastor Phillips. It was funny; he had a small desk set up for me with a small wood plaque. The plaque read "Josiah Whitby, Assistant Pastor." It was deeds like this that showed the true heart of our pastor. He was truly a kind man, but was a bit harsh when he preached. He had hardened somewhat following the death of his wife about 6 years earlier.

Today was Saturday, so I helped Pastor Phillips set up the church for the next day's services and he reviewed parts of his sermon with me. He asked me for input, but I mostly agreed with his fire and brimstone message. Although my preaching style would probably turn out to be much softer than his, I was in no position to question his effectiveness at saving the lost.

I departed just before sunset. The tree frogs were beginning their nightly chorus. It is amazing how a creature so small can unite with thousands of others to make a sound that cannot be ignored.

As I rode past the cemetery, I could not help but feel a little spooked. I know that I should "fear not," but I have been a little unnerved by that cemetery since I was a child.

Upon returning that next morning, the congregation was treated to another sermon by Pastor Phillips. When he was at his best, like today, he was the best preacher on earth. He knew the misdeeds of all of the parishioners so he would tailor his message to a particular person who was being unfaithful or who stole or was acting jealous. He would look down from the pulpit over his spectacles and say something like "The Bible says stealing is wrong, it's a sin. Now is there a man, woman, or child here who wants to tell me that it is not, hmmm?" He would drag out the hmmm as he looked at the suspects in the pews.

At the end of the service, Pastor Phillips reintroduced me to the congregation. Most of them did not recognize me since I had not been home for several years. He stated that I would be helping run the church and in a few years, if I was up to it, I may get to preach one Sunday a month.

Following that confidence-sparing endorsement, Pastor Phillips and I thanked the congregation as they left. It was great to see some familiar faces although I did not have the chance to greet everyone.

I did overhear one of the parishioners inviting Pastor Phillips to a harvest celebration on Tuesday. It was Zacharius Prose, one of the wealthiest plantation owners on Johns Island. He had thousands of acres of land and nearly 50 slaves. Following his invitation to Pastor Phillips, he turned and invited me and my family to attend as well. We were often invited to his house, but my parents usually found an excuse not to attend. We were in a different economic class than the Prose family. I had played with their daughter at some church picnics as a child, but I did not like Kelley Prose very much at the time. She was faster than me. It was a little embarrassing to be outrun by a girl.

Upon exiting the church, I did catch the eye of Kelley Prose riding in her father's carriage. It was a surreal moment. As if things moved at half speed before returning to normal. There was something about her. Something there. As was the case with other recent events in my life, the sight of her seemed to have a bigger meaning. Almost a purpose.

The next few days were uneventful. I was somewhat excited about attending an event at the Prose plantation. I was in a different position than I had previously been. I was welcome at these celebrations as a pastor. It is always hard to tell if people really want the pastor at a party like this or if they feel like they need to be liked by the pastor.

PROSE

On that Tuesday afternoon, I prepared to attend the evening celebration at the Prose plantation. My parents would attend this time as well, but I planned to travel separately, maybe as a sign of my independence. I do not know why. I did feel the need to show my future congregation that I was grown up now, independent. It just seemed like the right thing to do.

The trip over was enjoyable. I always have enjoyed the road toward their place. It is lined with live oak trees that create a canopy over the road. As a child, I called it the tunnel. The road was in good shape. One of the positive things about not having to pay your labor was that you could get them to do the jobs no one else wanted to.

As I turned through the gate onto the Prose property, several servants greeted me. Servant was a fancy word for slave. There were several old black women that offered us fresh lemonade. It was a nice treat for the trip up the long drive to the front of the house. Off in the distance, you could see a row of slave quarters flanked by a pecan tree grove. Most slave owners tried to present their servants as well-taken-care-of when others were around. I guess it meant that you had enough wealth to take care of your family as well as your slaves. It was funny how these days the thought of slaves and slavery transcended all of my thoughts whereas I had never really given it a second thought a year before.

The Prose house was even more magnificent than I had remembered. It was brick with several large columns lining the front porch. The trim was painted with a fresh white coat of paint. The porch was lined with imported wicker furniture. Tables were set up throughout the grounds with food and beverages. It was clear that they were expecting a large crowd.

As I pulled my carriage to the front of the house, an African boy took the reigns and said, "I will hitch these fo ya, mista." He could not have been more that 10. Again, I was offered a lemonade or a cocktail. I obviously opted for the lemonade. Although I had tasted of strong drink in my younger days, it was not something I was drawn to. In addition, it would not be appropriate for me to partake of such beverages, being the new pastor in town.

I meandered through the small groups of attendees, introducing and re-introducing myself. Most of the people I saw were parishioners of our church, but not all. There were the obligatory discussions of the North trying to outlaw slavery. This topic was sure to generate some less than Christian words. Most believed that eventually the South would sever its ties with the North and form its own country.

The root of all of these discussions was the desire to maintain slavery. Many supported slavery because they knew no other way. Others feared that they could not compete without the low cost labor, noting that the cost of the slave was the only cost to most slave owners. It must be pointed out that to say the only cause of Southern anger towards the North was slavery would be naïve.

Southerners just do not like other people telling them how to live their life. They love their laidback lifestyle. The slower pace. The land, the farms. It was always interesting to speak to a Northerner who moved to Charleston. Most would not leave our beloved city if their life depended on it. The lifestyle is infectious. You become it. One stroll down the streets of Ansonborough, a Charleston suburb, and most feel a connection. A stroll down the Battery. A visit to the Barrier Islands. The South is different. Southerners are different. We resist change for change's sake. Something new is not inherently better. In most cases, progress and modernization bring with them a host of problems as great as the remedy. This defiant stubbornness may be the biggest asset or detriment to the South's survival.

I caught the eye of Kelley at the party. At that time she was across the yard, sitting in the garden with some other young ladies. I did not get the chance to speak with her at that time due to the constant questioning from my parishioners. As a minister, you get a lot of philosophical questions that are difficult to answer in a yes or no fashion.

Pastor Phillips confronted me with a large beverage in his hand. It was clear that he had tasted a few strong beverages.

"Reverend Whitby, is it alright for me to take a drink of beer or whiskey?" He went on, "Even Jesus drank wine in the Bible. Heck, He even made it."

This drew a chuckle from those around him. While I do not believe he was looking for a serious response, I said, "Well, I always support people behaving more like Jesus." This too drew a laugh from the Pastor and those gathered around.

Eventually I made my way to Kelley. She was dressed all in white with a large brimmed hat. I must say she took my breath. She took my thoughts. She took me. Being a minister, one is rarely at a loss for words. In reality, most people wish we would talk less. Especially on Sunday mornings.

I collected my thoughts and said, "You want to race? I figure I can take you in that long dress." I promptly had to apologize. "That did not sound appropriate; I am sorry. I just remember how you would always outrun me at the church picnics. I have never really recovered from the embarrassment," I said with a smile.

"Well, Pastor Whitby, I am not nearly as fast as I used to be," Kelley said in a confident Southern drawl. That may be the one thing I like most about the South. The way the ladies talk. She went on, "You could probably catch me now."

I believe I turned a bit red-faced upon her response. At that time, I was not sure what she meant, but I was quite intrigued nonetheless. As I pondered her comments and fumbled for an eloquent response, she simply stared at my eyes. Before I could muster any words, I heard a loud shrill coming from the drive of the Prose property. One of the slave women was running down the road screaming.

"Help me, help me, she's on my back! She tryin' to get me! Help!" she cried in mortal fear.

I did not see anyone else around her. The African woman appeared to be alone.

One of the supervisors of Mr. Prose's plantation ran up to the slave woman and slapped her. I must admit, it makes me cringe when I see someone abuse another human like that, but that was the time we lived in and it was considered quite a humiliation for a slave to interrupt a gathering such as this.

The African woman could not be calmed through violence or discussion. I offered my services, having had some minor training in counseling at Seminary in aiding those that are distraught. I took the woman over behind the slave quarters so she would not run the risk of more abuse if she were crying out loudly.

"What is wrong? I asked. "Who is trying to get you?"

The woman paused her heavy panting and crying and looked me dead in the eye. This was no ordinary stare; it was the look of honest fear. She said, "Dat hag, she after me."

A hag was the subject of many old-time African folklore stories. She was an evil spirit that lived in the woods. She would come out every now and again and chase down folks wandering around at night. It was often referred to as having a "hag riding on your back." There was always some debate as to the true origin of the story. Some said the white folks made it up to keep the slaves from trying to escape at night; others said the story was an old tale from the African mainland. Still others said that it was tied to the old Indian tribes that lived on Johns Island years ago. Nevertheless, everyone believed that there was an element of truth to the stories and no one liked to travel around these parts at night alone.

After calming the African woman down and leaving her in the care of some other slaves, I returned to the festivities. I did not get another chance to talk to Kelley that night. It seemed she was tied up with discussions with her friends. Kelley's parents were quite protective of her and she was generally quite shy. I did, however, have the chance to tell the African woman's hag tale to a few guests. Most people dismissed it as legend, but you could tell they would sleep with one eye open that night.

As I told Pastor Phillips about the slave woman's story, he seemed a bit concerned. He said, "You know the Bible speaks of evil spirits in this world. I think we all should get our mind right. You never know what is lurking out there in them woods." He went on, "I think I will preach on that next Sunday." Pastor Phillips would never pass up the opportunity to put a little fear in the minds of the parishioners.

An evening wind began to blow, so many of us prepared to leave. Pastor Phillips and I followed one another in our respective carriages. We separated at the large Oak Tree that many called the "Angel Oak." Pastor Phillips headed toward the church where his home was located and I headed back to my folks' house. It was dark and a thunderstorm was looming. My parents had come home early and were already in bed. I crept inside so as to not wake them. I crawled in bed and quickly fell into a deep sleep.

The next thing I remember was running. Running as fast as I could through the woods. It must have been a dream, but no dream has ever felt so real. It was the kind of dream when you can touch, smell, and feel things. There was the sound of something behind me. Perhaps a wild hog, or a man, I really wasn't sure. Next I felt something holding on to each shoulder, and I could not shake it loose. I ran and ran and ran, but it was no use. I heard a wispy voice in my ear. "Do right, Preacher Man, do right." As I turned to look over my shoulder, I saw the face of an old woman. Her skin was a gray color. Her hair, stringy like the Spanish moss that grows in the live oak trees. Her breath had a stench of marsh mud. I instantly awoke.

I was wet from head to toe as if I had been out in the storm that had just passed. I am still not sure if the wetness was sweat or if I had wet myself. I was shaking with fear. I do not know if this was real or just a dream. I had encountered a "hag." Now I know why that African woman looked the way she looked at the Prose house. I did not sleep any more on that night. I was shaken. I cannot remember feeling this way since I was a young child that was afraid of the dark.

PASTOR

AS THE SUN ROSE, I cleaned myself up and went outside to look about. I saw Mamie preparing breakfast in the kitchen outside of our home. I approached her and said, "Mamie, have you ever seen a hag? Have you ever had one riding your back? Are they real?"

Mamie stopped me and said, "Whoa, child, one question at a time. The answer is yes, dey real, and yes I seen one, but no I ain't never had one ridin' my back. Folks don't always live to tell about that. Once dat hag catches you, she takes your skin and leaves nothing but a pile of bones."

Mamie went on, "Sit down, child, and I will tell you of that hag. The Hag is a spirit, like a ghost or witch. She flies around at night looking for a new body to take over. She will sit on you while you sleep and suck your breath clean out. This gives her life. If you fight her or resist, she may then jus' take your skin for herself."

I was really shaken now. Mamie continued, "Sometimes she chases people through the woods or she will enter a person's house through a crack or open window at night. Hags are a peculiar lot though. They get distracted easy. They will sit and count all the bristles of a broom or brush or they may count the holes in a colander. Many folks put those things outside their house to help occupy a hag if she come by. That hag will get you if she wants you though. When she need a new skin, she gonna find it."

Mamie's story seemed a bit extreme. It made me hope that I had just had a nightmare. I was a bit relieved, because I was truly unnerved by that night. Following breakfast, I put on my pastor collar and hat and headed off to the church. I looked forward to collaborating with Pastor Phillips on Sunday's sermon. I planned to weave some of the "hag myth" into the conversation about his upcoming sermon, if he cared for input. Pastor Phillips always said, "Preserving souls is like preserving food—sometimes you use sugar and sometimes you use vinegar." I suppose the hag story would be considered a little dose of vinegar.

As I approached the church, I saw the pastor carriage parked adjacent to the cemetery. It appeared as though the good Pastor Phillips was sleeping in it. Not a surprise considering the wine he had consumed the night before. It was not common for him to consume alcohol, but he did on occasion. He was as much a man of the people and a friend as he was a preacher. I was a bit amused at the thought of his having been a little carefree with his lips and throat the night prior.

I walked up to the carriage calling his name; I did not want to frighten him. I was also concerned with causing him shame or embarrassment. It is not a measure of pride to have slept all night in your carriage during a storm. I shook the carriage from behind, but he still seemed to be sleeping. I approached the front of the carriage and saw that his eyes were wide open and his skin had a pale pallor to it. Then fear overtook my lightheartedness. Pastor Phillips was not breathing. I thought he was dead.

I screamed. What was I to do? I guess one's inner self takes over at this point. I immediately jumped onto my carriage and raced off to get Doctor Heaton. We returned a short time later to find no change. The doctor rushed to his side and after a cursory examination said, "It must have been his heart. It just gave out." Then he burst into tears. I had never seen a doctor cry, but he was very close to Pastor Phillips, as one would expect. Doctors and preachers worked very close together. A lot of the time when folks got sick, they did not make it long.

That day was one of the longest of my life. Countless people came by to see if it was true, had the Pastor really died? One family brought by a pine coffin to lay his body in. Others inquired about a funeral. A lot was put on me at that time. I had to arrange for the funeral service and burial.

I had to plan the funeral for the next afternoon. In those days, you had to bury folks quickly to avoid them beginning to get to stinking. My father sent Jackson, Mamie's husband, to help me dig the grave. I could have had other Africans help, but somehow I wanted to feel more of the hurt of losing the pastor. Each shovelful of dirt was a wrenching reminder of the loss. Looking back, I think some of my pain was the loss of the pastor and some was due to my fear of what it would mean to my life. I knew I may be asked to head the church and all the duties that come with it. That was clearly a selfish feeling. But in reality, most of the pain we feel when someone passes is selfish. We are sad that we will not have that person in our lives. The deceased are rarely sad, for they are on their way to heaven.

That night I did not sleep much, if any. I stayed at my desk in the church's basement writing a eulogy for my pastor and mentor. It is a very difficult thing to do—trying to summarize the meaning and importance of someone in a few short paragraphs. A person's life is so much more than that. A laugh, a sigh, a smile, a kind word, and even a stern word. These are the things that make people special, but we do not really even notice consciously.

The service itself and burial went well the next day. I was somewhat relieved that it was over. I managed not to embarrass myself with my speech, but I was overcome with tears a few times. Again, the nervousness coupled with my sadness was hard to mask. At the end of the burial, I was approached by several of the large landowners and contributors to the church. They asked me to stay on as the head pastor, which I graciously accepted. I did ask for their patience as I learned my new role. I was new to managing the business matters of a church as well as all of the political aspects.

Mr. Prose approached and stated, "I will be sending over a couple of my slaves to help you around here. They will be yours as long as you need them. In addition, my daughter Kelley will come by a few days a week to help with some of the church goings on."

While I did not like the concept of me managing Africans, I was in no position to say no. I also was a bit excited about the opportunity to see Kelley more often.

I graciously thanked everyone for their faith in me and for Mr. Prose's kind offerings. I then proceeded home for a good night's rest and some home cooking. I knew that tomorrow, I would have to begin my duties as head pastor. Life was about to take another turn. How many turns can one life take in a few weeks' period?

Maybe it was my blind faith or maybe it was blind ignorance, but I did feel that I was being led to the place I was meant to reside. Each day and each event were setting up my life's mission of helping others. Who the "others" were was what I had yet to discover.

Upon arrival at the church the next morning, sadness overtook me. It was quiet. I began the grim task of going through all of Pastor Phillips's papers and files that were stored in the basement and throughout the church. Luckily, he was a fairly organized man who did not keep an inordinate amount of old stuff. I did review many of his old sermons dating back to when I was a child. It was quite a memory-stirring event. There were also files on the church itself. Some of its founders and the architect were also noted.

I proceeded to clean out some of the storage closets as well. I wanted to start fresh as the new pastor. Getting rid of the memory of the former pastor was not my mission; I just felt like I needed to make the church mine. One of the storage closets in the back of the basement contained some old costumes from Easter pageants and the annual Christmas play. I even recognized a wise man robe that I had worn when I was 8.

My next discovery was even more interesting. At the back of this closet was another door. It appeared to have been blocked for years based on the dust and spider webs. The door was padlocked. After finding a ring of 100 or more keys, I was able to locate the correct key to open the door. Once opened, it revealed what appeared to be a dirt cave or path under the ground. Without much thought, I grabbed a candle and followed down the path. It led to a small room with a stairwell extending upward. Of course I went up and opened the overhead door. It revealed yet another small concrete room constructed of tabby, the combination of mortar and oyster shells that was most often used for durable buildings.

As I exited this small room I was outside in the cemetery. The closet had led me underground about 50 feet from the church and up through the crypt that Pastor Phillips had said was built for the Revolutionary War Veterans. He was right; there was no one buried in there.

I closed the doors back up and returned to the basement to review the blueprints. It appeared as though the underground path I had traveled was not on the original plan. I am guessing it was designed to give Revolutionary War soldiers an escape path if the British overcame them. No major battles took place on Johns Island, so I guessed the path was sealed up and never used. It was often a custom for soldiers to seek refuge in a church when necessary. A place of sanctuary, ideally.

I continued to review the various drawings and plans of the original church and its property. Wadmalaw Creek bordered the land to the East. It was a rather large marsh inlet that was full of crabs, fish, and shrimp. Much of what people on the island consumed came from the tidal creeks. The other side of the church property bordered the Prose plantation, although the house was several miles away.

Of note on one drawing of the church property was an area designated as the Slave Boneyard. I gathered that this was an old cemetery used for the slaves that had passed away. I took the papers outside and went looking for this area. I walked behind the church, through some of the trees and brush back to a small opening.

There it was. A small open area surrounded by a few large myrtles and live oaks. There were no discernable plots. Just a few old wooden crosses and a few headstones of granite. There were a few names etched into the markers. The boneyard seemed to be symbolic of slavery itself, impersonal. These individuals, these humans, were simply first names. Probably not even their given names, but a name that the slave owner used to get their attention. It was hard to explain the way I felt while standing in that cemetery. While I did not know anything about those buried there, I just felt that they deserved more. They were more important than some old stones and sticks covered in brush.

VISITORS

EARLY THE NEXT MORNING, I returned to the church, as would be my routine for potentially the rest of my life. There awaiting my arrival was a cart with two Africans sitting upon it. They said, "Pastor Josiah, Mr. Prose sents us on over to help you out. We supposed to stay here until you don't needs us no more. Even 5 years."

The couple was familiar. It was the old slave woman who had seen the Hag during the Proses' party as well as her husband. They were obviously a little older, which is why Mr. Prose was willing to part with them. I prefer the company of older individuals. They are typically wiser than those that demonstrate more fire than heat.

The old woman then looked at me and said, "You know dat hag still around here. Word has it dat's what killed the preacher. He seen the hag and it scared him clean to death. I bets his eyes was open when you found him."

I assured the woman that she would be safe here at the church. I said, "I do not know if that hag is real, but I do know that evil spirits do not want to come around a church. You will be safe here." I invited them both inside the sanctuary to get to know them better and let them know more about me.

"What are your names?" I said.

The man said, "I am Earl and dis here Charlotte."

"Good enough," I responded. "You can call me Pastor Josiah. Now let me tell you a little about myself," I said with some reservation. I knew I was about to confide in two people that I hardly knew, but they were the first people I felt like I could be completely honest with in the past month. "I think slavery is wrong. I do not mean that I think it is a bad idea, I mean it is wrong in the eyes of God. It is immoral and should be abolished."

It was clear that they did not know what to say. I am sure those are words that they had never heard spoken before. Not even a fellow slave would speak those words out loud for fear of repercussions.

I went on, "Now, I am not sure what to do about my beliefs. Obviously, I will keep you both here and I will need you to help me around the church. In exchange, I will give you room, board, and food. In addition, I will pay you a wage as I can afford it. Slavery will not be abolished any time soon, so we will do our best to help as many people as possible in the meantime. One person, one family at a time. I will try to change people's hearts with my sermons. But it is critical that we all understand that none of us can be upfront or vocal about our goals or we three will be hanging from trees. I will be in the middle and you two on either side."

Earl looked at me and said, "I trust you, Pastor. I don't know why, but I trust you."

Later that day, I showed Earl and Charlotte the Slave Boneyard and asked if they would be interested in helping me clean it up some. Make it look proper. We would have to do this in our spare time because I needed to clean out Pastor Phillips's house, clean out the basement of the church, and begin preparing for my Sunday sermon.

That afternoon was spent going through Pastor Phillips's home. We pulled out all of his old clothes and put them in a box to use for the less fortunate or for those that experience hardship. Most of the furniture would remain for my use. The house was nice but a little dirty since Mrs. Phillips had passed. Men are not known for their tidiness.

That night Charlotte prepared a nice meal. It was amazing the way she cooked. Over dinner, we talked. I felt as though we were equals. That's because we were. We talked about their lives, their hardships, and the future.

Charlotte said, "The worst thing I ever did live through was them taking my baby. They took him when he was 5 and sold him to someone else. I never seen him since. I guess he would be 20 now. I hope he is well. One day, I gonna find him. That will be a great day."

I wondered if anyone else had ever heard this story, if anyone cared. It brought me to tears. My sister was taken from me when she was just 5 and I still have not recovered fully. I do not discuss it with anyone. It is a dark place deep in my soul. I have to leave it there.

To have your child taken from you by another for no real reason other than money would be agony. There were always those that tried to justify slavery based on Biblical stories, but there is no one who could ever justify splitting families. Taking babies from their mothers. That ain't right now or ever.

The conversation turned a little more practical and strategic after that.

"I need to help people. We will just call the slaves 'people' for simplicity and accuracy." I said. "I will find a way to do it. I just need to be careful. I, or shall I say we, may only help one or two people in our lifetime, but we will help nonetheless. We cannot act rash or careless for that will clear the road to trouble. Let us do our daily chores and we will know when the time is upon us."

The next morning we began to clean the basement of the church. We laughed at some of the costumes the children wore in plays. I also showed Charlotte and Earl the secret passage that led to the crypt and the cemetery. They were both quite afraid. The Africans, generally speaking, were more superstitious. Spirits were more a part of their African heritage. I can honestly say that I was a little more fearful of sprits following my dream of the Hag.

Charlotte was a funny old lady. Almost every conversation or situation that would arise, she would blame it on the Hag. She would say, "You hear that thunder? Dat hag comin'," or "You see that black bird? He a friend of that hag." It was all quite entertaining. In the short time I had been around those two, I really began to enjoy their company. We were somewhat dependent on each other. In life many people talk about the

"Golden Rule." It is based on a Biblical passage that states that you should treat others the way you want to be treated. I have also heard tell of a "Platinum Rule" which says to treat others the way they want to be treated. It's a small difference that can make a big difference.

Later that morning, a carriage pulled up being driven by an African man. In the back of the carriage was Kelley Prose. Her father had sent her, as promised. The carriage driver handed me a note that said,

"Pastor Whitby, please look after our daughter and let her assist in some duties around the church. We have grown concerned at the many number of suitors pursuing her and wish for her to be sheltered from the over-zealous youth of the island. If there is any Biblical truth you can put in her to help her live right, please do so. Sincerely, Zacharius Prose."

I found the note quite interesting since I had become quite enamored with that Kelley myself. It was a fact, however, that she would most likely be safer around me than many of my peers on the island. While I had the same yearnings and lusts as all others, I would suppress them until marriage. It is the right thing to do for everyone, but especially for a pastor who must lead by example.

I greeted Kelley with a smile and brought her up to date on what myself, Earl, and Charlotte had been doing around the church. I obviously could not tell her everything about our conversations as well as our potential work on the Slave Boneyard. I did not know Kelley very well at this time. With her father being one of the wealthiest slave owners on the island, I would have to be careful. For now, my anti-slavery leanings would have to be buried.

    Kelley was a pleasant young woman. Very friendly and personable. Always smiling. She loved to laugh and joke. I believe that may have been the concern of her parents. Her light-hearted nature came across as a little flirtatious. She was very smart and organized. Over the next few days, we organized the church files, created a daily schedule for me, and planned a trip to Charleston for supplies. The church was in order based upon the stewardship of Pastor Phillips, but I would be doing things a little differently. Not better, just different.

    I did not see Kelley for the next two days; I was busy writing my first sermon. Earl and Charlotte were cleaning up around the church and also working on straightening up the boneyard. It was challenging to develop a sermon so close to the death of the previous pastor. I wanted to convey the message that change can be good, in this case, the change being a new pastor. My soul yearned to preach a "Love One Another" message, but this was not the time. I would have to earn their trust before I could change their hearts. My goal was to use my sermons to help my mission. That is what preachers always seek to do, use stories to get people to think their way.

    On that Sunday, Kelley and her family sat on the front row of pews. That added to the already high level of nervousness that I had worked up. In Seminary, we gave practice sermons, but nothing prepares you for the real thing. A hundred sets of eyes looking at you. Complete quiet as you approach.

As I actually did approach the podium, I stepped on a loose board. It made a moaning or a creaking sound. Not at all unlike a human's passing of foul gas. There were some slight chuckles by a few in the audience; I did not know exactly what to say. I turned flushed and uttered the first thing that came to mind: "Change can be good; I plan to change the position of this podium before next week." That drew a soothing laugh from the congregation. From that point on, I felt like I was among friends and I could teach with ease. The sermon was not lengthy. I tried to make a few points without putting the congregation to sleep. I once heard a pastor at Seminary say, "No one ever complains about getting home early on a Sunday morning."

The following Monday, Kelley returned early. This was the day that we planned to go into Charleston to buy new supplies for the church. There was a significant amount of money that the church had. The folks on Johns Island were quite generous with their donations and Pastor Phillips had been a wise steward of their money.

Typically, an unmarried man and woman would not travel together into Charleston. It just did not look right. But the fact that I wore my pastor collar and the presence of Earl and Charlotte in the cart following close behind made the situation look better for Kelley. The trip into Charleston took about 3 hours. It was the first time I had ever really had the chance to get to know Kelley. See a deeper side of her. I think it was on that trip that I first fell in love with her.

The road to Charleston was often called Rockville Trail because it was the major road between the small fishing village of Rockville and the city of Charleston. It was rather a scenic route. It was lined with many large live oak trees that had large amounts of moss hanging down. The road was nicely shaded and surrounded by large thickets of myrtles and palmettos. There were several large farms and plantations along the way as well as several bridges that crossed a large marsh inlet.

At first, both Kelley and I were quiet. A little shy I guess, but then she abruptly asked, "So why did you want to become a pastor?"

I sensed a little disappointment in her voice. So I replied, "Kelley, I am a pastor, not a priest. I can marry, have children, and all the other things lay people do. I just am called to behave as a role model for others. I must uphold my faith." That reply was probably inappropriate. Kelley did not want to know if I could marry her, only my motivation for going to Seminary. "But to get to your question," I quickly redirected, "I have always wanted to help people. To make them feel better. To give them peace in their life. To help husbands and wives get along. To help people cherish their children. I guess I am an idealist. I believe that one person can make a difference. Maybe not change the whole world, but change one person's world." After that long and fancy answer, I finished, "Plus I like the neat hat and collar I get to wear."

Kelley laughed and then said, "There is more to you than I expected. I hope you accomplish your mission in life."

I then asked Kelley, "So what do you want out of life? Do you hope to have a large plantation like your father?"

Kelley looked down and said, "I just want to be happy, truly happy. My parents have the whole world, but I don't see passion in their eyes. I don't mean lust. I mean passion for life. I want to have children and have fun with them. Ride horses, go fishing, play at the beach. I want to enjoy this lovely world that we live in. I know life isn't always fun or easy but I want it to always be enjoyable."

I think I loved her from then on. She was everything I was not. I was more serious. I worried about the world's problems. I pondered solutions. She just wanted to give everyone a hug and laugh with them. I would learn that both approaches work. A hug is a short-term treatment that satisfies until a long-term cure can be found.

I felt the attraction between Kelley and myself was mutual, but I was willing to watch how things developed. Many women are not interested in a pastor because we typically have a lower income than others and we are tied to a stricter code of behavior. I once heard it told that a pastor has "all of the responsibilities of a doctor at one-third the pay." This phrase was not entirely inaccurate.

The approach to Charleston gave me a thrill. I must admit I love this city. The beautiful homes, restaurants, and shops were a pleasure to see. I believe it to be the most romantic city in the world. It is a lot like a shy woman. A very beautiful, stately outward appearance with a seductive, flirtatious interior.

Charleston was a multi-faceted city. There were some houses of ill repute and a few saloons, but overall it was a city of merchants, hotels, and restaurants. The recent arrival of the railroads as well as the continued use of the seaport had made Charleston a rather wealthy city. The plantation owners were still a dominant force in Charleston even though a base of manufacturing had begun to take hold.

Our fine city was overlooked by much of the world. It did not have the reputation of the larger cities such as New York or London. We liked it that way. The city was, however, extremely historic. Charleston was an innovator in many areas. I, like most others in this area, were taught during our schooling about the things that made our great city special.

British settlers originally founded Charleston in 1670. It was originally called Charles Towne in honor of King Charles II of England. Some of the founding documents for the Carolina colony ensured religious freedom for all. This concept was fairly unique in the world at that time. It helped Charleston draw a diverse population of Jews, Catholics, and Protestants, which further enriched the Charleston culture. This city is believed to be the birthplace of Reformed Judaism.

Charleston was the original capital of Carolina. Later the colony was divided into North and South Carolina and then the capital of South Carolina was moved to Columbia. By 1700, Charleston was a major trading center. It had also established one of the first tax-supported libraries in America. Charleston also had a more adventurous side. Several pirates including Blackbeard and Stede Bonnet sailed through these parts in the early 1700s. Twenty-nine of these pirates were later captured and hanged for public viewing.

Charleston was also a pioneer in business and the arts. The Dock Street Theater, the Charleston Museum, and the Chamber of Commerce were some of the first of their kind in the country. Due to the significant number of fires in the city, Charlestonians organized the first fire insurance company in America. Many of the institutions we take for granted today were created right here.

Our city also found itself in the middle of the Revolutionary War. The British were having minimal luck in defeating America's troops up North, so they shifted their campaign towards the South. Charleston was the major center of commerce in the South at the time. British troops surrounded the city from the North and landed on Seabrook Island from the sea. Eventually the South Carolina militia took back most of the state as the war came to an end.

During the 1800s, Charleston became home to the first medical school in the South. The presence of the Medical College of South Carolina brought premier medical care close to home. The railroad entered Charleston, allowing for a greater inflow and outflow of products and people. This led to the rapid growth and placed our city in the state it is today. A city with all of the hope and promise of the future, but the weight of slavery holding it back.

The city, in some regards, was being pulled by two forces. Some wanted to maintain Charleston as a slavery-centered city that would wall off the rest of the world. The other forces wanted to modernize Charleston with a focus on manufacturing and the arts. Both forces were uniquely Southern and neither wanted to become like the North. Charleston has often been described as a dichotomy. It seems to always have two opposing views that dance together in perfect rhythm.

As we strolled along East Bay and Market Street, I felt perfect. I had a lovely lady at my side and I was in the most beautiful city in the world. Charleston just makes you feel a little more content. Life slows a little. Satisfaction is achieved by just looking around.

Kelley asked, "What are all those pineapples and fruit doing on the front porches of many of the houses?"

I actually knew the answer to this. It always makes a man feel good when he can be a source of knowledge or information. "It's a tradition that when a seaman returns home from a voyage, he brings exotic produce from the islands he has visited. The fruit tells the neighbors that the seaman has returned and that they are welcome to come over to enjoy the fresh produce. The pineapple, in particular, has become a symbol of hospitality."

Kelley seemed amused by the story thus far.

I continued, "There is another version of this story as well. Some say that the seaman's wives would put the produce on the front porch to alert their boyfriends that their husband had returned. It served as a warning not to come around."

Kelley laughed shyly. "That would be clever although highly immoral."

Kelley and I went into one of the large mercantile stores to buy the items we needed for the church. A few new Bibles, paper, ink, and some pencils. All of the things that help our church work. Everything a person could ever need was available in this city.

We proceeded down by the old market, the slave market to be more precise. Contrary to the name, this market was never used for the selling of slaves. It was a market where slaves were allowed to sell their goods if permitted by their owners. It was now being utilized as an open market for goods and produce. Slave trading had been formally banned and then reinstated multiple times. Currently, it was illegal to import slaves and sell them. But that did not stop individual slave owners from trading them informally at local markets.

Upon finishing our business in Charleston, we had lunch at a small restaurant overlooking the bay. We then took the long route out of the city. We circled around the waterfront park. The most beautiful homes in Charleston are aligned one after another along this road. We looked out over Ft. Sumter, a peaceful fort in the Charleston Bay that had not seen any action since the Revolutionary War. Many couples were strolling along the waterfront. You do not walk in Charleston. You stroll. The term walking is too simple for Charleston. It was romantic. We left downtown Charleston and headed back down Rockville Trail toward Johns Island.

As we left the outskirts of downtown Charleston, we passed one of those unofficial slave markets. A few white gentlemen were haggling over the trade of a slave family. Once we got a little closer, we witnessed one of the most painful experiences I have ever seen. A slave family was being split up for sale. The parents were sent with one plantation owner and the two children were being sent to another. I could hear Charlotte whimpering in the cart behind us. I was nearly driven to tears as well. This was the root of the evil in slavery. Clear disregard for other humans. These slave traders were clearly not "loving their neighbor as themselves."

The last sight we saw before pulling around the next corner was the mother of this slave family giving her daughter a doll. It appeared to be a handmade doll of cloth and sweetgrass. The mother said, "You keep this; it will remind you of me until we are together again."

I was curious as to Kelley's reaction, so I glanced over to her.

She appeared shocked, almost in disbelief. "Do they routinely do these things? Separate mammas and babies?"

"Every day," I said.

"It is painful to see. Surely there is a better way to handle such matters," Kelley said. I do not think she had ever contemplated an end to slavery, but she did see the inhumanity of it on that day. I did not discuss the slavery issue with Kelley any more that day. Before we left the market area, however, I did turn to Earl and Charlotte and gave them a wink. I was going to do something about those children's sadness. I was going to make it right.

Kelley and I talked very little for the rest of the trip. The images of those children being taken from their parents was burned into my brain. I was reviewing it over and over. An African child's tears were the same as yours or mine. That pain is real. It cannot be minimized by a title such as slave or property.

Upon our return to the church, Kelley's carriage was awaiting to take her back home. We parted ways for that day. I requested that she come back as often as she could because I needed the extra help. At a minimum I could use her on the coming Friday and Saturday to help me prepare the church for Sunday services. In reality, I did not need her help, but I was in need of her presence. I was becoming quite smitten with that young woman. And this time I planned on catching her.

PLAN

ON THAT EVENING, I had dinner with Earl and Charlotte as I had become accustomed to. They were both very quiet. Not a word was spoken. I knew the events of the day, specifically the slave sale, brought back incredibly painful memories. It was almost unthinkable to imagine them having gone through a similar traumatic event. I looked up at both of them and said, "We are gonna get those folks back their kids."

Both Earl and Charlotte nearly choked on their dinner. "You crazy, Pastor. What you gonna do? Steal them kids in the night and take the whole family up North?" Earl said.

"If that's what it takes, we will, or shall I say I will. I am going to figure out a way to help people, those people. If you all would like to help me that would be great. If not, I would kindly ask you to help me keep my efforts a secret."

I knew I wouldn't be able to make the slavery situation right in one day, but I would make a plan to fix this injustice. I cannot change the world, but I could change those kids' world. At this point, I began to care less about my own well-being and more about others. This is the true teaching of Jesus. In an odd way, the more I went against society's teachings, the more I was upholding Jesus' teachings.

I asked Earl and Charlotte to help me come up with a plan to help those kids and when I figured out how to do it safely, I would. We went off to bed that night. I felt a little better at that point. I always feel better when I am doing something or planning to do something rather than sitting around doing nothing. I awoke early the next morning. I had a reason to rise. I was on a mission.

Several days passed without much talk about the separated slave family. I did not know if I had scared Earl and Charlotte. They could surely be killed and I would not fare much better if we were caught helping slaves escape. I am not sure if I was driven by a higher power or my youthful ignorance, but I was not fearful. It just seemed like the right thing to do.

On Wednesday evening during dinner, things were very quiet. I sensed that something was going on in their minds. Finally Earl spoke up. "Pastor Josiah, we's gonna help you. We's gonna help dat family. No one should be without their children. We may die tryin' but that's better than living for nothing at all I suppose. I don't really have a plan, but we do gots some ideas." He went on, "We've been working down at that ol' slave cemetery and finding lots of bones."

Charlotte chimed in, "I think dat ol' hag been down there eatin' supper."

"Well, that ol' hag may just be the one who can help us," Earl continued. "Most folks around here believe in that hag. I sure do. I know she's real. I know she don't come around often and she sure wouldn't do us a favor. Maybe we can pretends like the Hag took the children and they could just disappear. Only bones would be found after that."

I was impressed. "Earl, you just might have something there. It just may work. Most white folks believe in the Hag legend, and recent sightings have surely got people a little on edge. Let's study on that. I could preach this Sunday's sermon on demons and evil spirits as they are mentioned in the Bible. That would get them thinking about it. The Devil and his workers are all around," I said with a sense of intrigue. I had no intention of lying to people or betraying my faith. I would preach with 100% pure Biblical accuracy, but I would utilize my teachings to further my goals. There's nothing wrong with that.

I asked Earl and Charlotte to find out what plantations the separated parents and children had been taken to. The Africans had a communication network that no one could figure out. They talked to one another and kept in touch with others without the white folks' knowing. Our goal was to reunite the family before summer's end. If they were to have a chance to get up North or out West, it would have to be done before winter. And before the leaves had fallen from the trees.

We also planned to utilize the old crypt and underground tunnel as a hiding place for the family until we could help them head to freedom. We all knew that we could just get them back together and then point them in the right direction; the rest would be up to God and their own efforts.

Charlotte demanded that the roof of the underground tunnel and crypt be painted a sky blue color. The Africans called the color "haint blue." The word "haint" was a mispronunciation of the word "haunt." It was supposed to look like the color of the daytime sky. It was believed that most spirits, including the Hag, would not come out during the day. If the spirit looked up and saw the sky blue color, even at night, they would run away. The use of this color paint became customary in Charleston. Whether there was any truth to the story no one knows. But I was all for having a little extra protection from whatever evil forces may come our way.

I began to focus on my sermons. They were becoming more and more a tool to help our plan work. From time to time, I felt a little deceitful, utilizing God's Word to carry out a secret plan. In reality, I was utilizing God's Word to help two little children hopefully spend the rest of their lives with their mother and father. It's funny how the difference between evil and good can be a few simple words.

As the weekend approached, it was time for Kelley to return to help us. It was difficult to stay focused on our plan when she was around. She made it difficult for me to concentrate. I did not want to do anything but look at her and hear her talk. Everyone speaks of love, but words can't describe that feeling. A feeling by definition should be the inability to put into words what you are experiencing.

Kelley began to warm toward me as well. We would exchange glances and then turn away with a slight blush. She helped make my new home, the pastor's house, seem friendlier. She placed flowers around. Helped rearrange the furnishings. She had a flair for making things seem better.

On Saturday evening Kelley proceeded back home again. I hated to see her go, but I needed to practice my sermon and get mentally prepared for the challenges of the next day. Earl, Charlotte, and I had dinner and I told them about some of the parts of the sermon. Charlotte cried out, "Child, don't tell me these stories just before bed. That's when they come out. The hags, devils, witches. Save those stories for tomorrow."

Earl seemed a little shaken as well. It was hard to tell if he was really concerned with evil spirits or just concerned that he may not get a good night's rest if Charlotte was scared. If mama ain't happy, ain't nobody happy. Truer words have never been spoken.

The next morning the parishioners began to arrive right on time. Many would have a few of their slaves drive them in the carriages. The slaves would then sit outside the church and listen to the sermon as best they could. I planned to open a few extra windows to be sure that everyone was a little uneasy on Johns Island. In order for our plan to work, folks had to believe that the Hag was out there and that she would catch folks.

"Welcome, friends, welcome," I began. "Today's sermon will be on the darker side of this world. There is evil all around in this world. We need to know this as we go about our daily activities. The Devil and his legion of evil spirits are everywhere. They tempt us, lead us to destruction, and cause foul words to fly from our mouths."

Following several more Biblical stories concerning spirits, I mentioned the Hag.

"Recently here on Johns Island, many folks have claimed to see a hag. As most of you know the Hag is believed to be a witch or a demonic spirit that roams these woods. She comes out every once in a while to get herself a soul. She chases you down, jumps on your back, and then eats you alive. Most of the time only bones are left."

I could see many in the pews squirming a little. They knew of the Hag stories and believed them. They were fearful.

I went on, "Now I do not know if these hags are real and I do not know if she really lives here on Johns Island. I do know that the Devil works in mysterious ways so we all need to be good and trust in God. That is the only way to be safe from evil."

Having sufficiently scared the congregation, I concluded the service. Hopefully I scared them to behave a little better but also laid a foundation for our plan to succeed. We still did not know the exact location of the slave children and their parents that we were going to reunite. That may take a few days.

On Monday, I asked Charlotte to make some pies for many of the local plantation owners in the area. Earl and I would deliver the pies as a good will gesture from the church. It never hurt to do a little something extra for those that helped the church stay afloat. The real goal, however, was to allow Earl and myself to look around at the different plantations to see if we could find the family. I could deliver the pies while Earl watered the horses and interacted with those slaves. He could ask questions to try and locate those kids and their parents.

But he would have to be careful because not every slave was willing to talk to someone they did not know very well. I relied on Earl's experience and judgment.

Upon leaving the Walker property, Earl said, "I think I know where the kids are. Just a few miles down the road at the Davis plantation towards Rockville. It's close to the church. The parents are right here. Right here at the Walker place."

This was ideal that both the parents and the kids were nearby. Real close to the church. We really did not have a back-up plan in case they were far away. The Lord was with us on this one.

We tentatively planned to reunite the family on that Friday night and help them get on their way up North. Again, I never once stopped to think this was foolish or risky. I was very naïve. These actions could have gotten us all killed. How would I feel, being responsible for the deaths of that family, Earl, and Charlotte? But of course, in that case I probably wouldn't have too long of a chance to feel much at all.

We would have to come up with a way to tell the slave parents what we were planning without anyone else finding out. We were not even sure that they would want to take such a risk, based on the painful cries we already heard upon the separation of that family. I also saw the pain Charlotte had felt when talking about having her son taken years before. Those wounds never heal.

Earl and I decided to go back to all of the plantations on Wednesday of that week to let them know the topic of next Sunday's sermon. We said it would be on the Ten Commandments. Folks always love sermons on that because they think in their mind about the people they know who are covetous, thieves, and adulterers. My hope was that we could fill the church. The more people that were at the church meant the fewer that were looking for the escapees.

Tuesday was a great day; I once again had the pleasure of Kelley's company. More and more we would just sit around and talk. We would always start out doing some chore around the church but then find ourselves talking about life, our dreams, our childhood, or the world in general. These conversations were very lighthearted in nature. It was a welcomed escape from the other tasks pulling at my mind and heart. Kelley was everything you would want in a partner. The one that sets your mind at ease. A calming force.

We went on a picnic that day. I actually had prepared a lunch and we headed down by the marsh under a large oak tree. We spread a large blanket and took in the salty air and the cool breeze blowing in from the water. Following the meal, I leaned against the old tree and Kelley leaned back against me. This was the first time we had physically touched one another. It was lustful contact. She was simply leaning back against my chest. It felt right. I was supporting her. That's what I was meant to do. We sat there for what seemed like hours, talking.

I did muster up the courage to ask Kelley about our future. If she thought we might formally court. Would she ever be interested in pursuing a long-term relationship? We also talked about her father and what he might think of her being involved with a pastor. Southern society at that time was very similar to other wealthy societies throughout the world. The daughters were typically wedded to the sons of other wealthy landowners. Love was secondary to wealth and power.

I also asked Kelley about her thoughts on slavery. I inquired, "Do you think slavery is right? Is it good for one man to own another? Is it right in God's eyes? Is it right to separate families? Is it—"

"Well, Josiah, are you gonna let me answer the questions?" Kelley interrupted.

"I do apologize," I said. "I am just a little confused now. Being a pastor means that I have to look at things differently. I have to follow God's rules first as all men should do."

"I will answer your question. Does it pain me when I see a slave getting beaten or sold or their kids sold? Absolutely. One would have to be pure evil not to feel some compassion. I just do not know what the alternative is. We have never known a world without slaves so I guess we are scared of what we have never seen or known. The evil behind slavery is the greed. Men want land, money, and power. That is why they desire free slave labor. They value those things over humanity."

At that point I saw a side of Kelley that I had not seen. She was not only beautiful on the outside but was very thoughtful on the inside. I knew at some point I would tell her of my efforts to help the slave family and my longer term goal of helping as many slaves as possible to have a better life. I, or perhaps we, may never see slavery abolished, but we could try to help people and do right.

Kelley added, "I think we all want a perfect world, but we cannot stop living while we wait on that to occur."

"You are brilliant, Kelley Prose, and lovely as well," I said. I believe I made her blush a bit.

That picnic concluded and we both headed back to the church. It was time for Kelley to head back home. I needed to spend some time with Earl to figure out if our plan would work. Friday was only a few days away and we had to be ready.

MISSION

THE NEXT DAY, WEDNESDAY, Earl and I went around to all of the houses and plantations around the church. Our outward mission was to invite everyone to church on Sunday, but the reality was that we needed to somehow let both the slave parents and children know what they needed to do on Friday night. I trusted Earl to get a message to the slaves. He was able to speak to a few of them as I talked to the landowners. We made a pretty good team. Looking back, this was just another example of the risks we took. We really did not think through many of our decisions. I consider it blind faith, and we were being led to do this, but at what price?

Later that day, Earl, Charlotte, and I had a chance to sit down and discuss the details of the plan. Earl told me that both the slave parents and the slave children would leave out of their plantations at midnight and run as fast as they could up the main roads toward the intersection of Main Road and Rockville Road. The church was located near that intersection. Once they neared that area we would do the rest.

In those days there was minimal security at night to keep the slaves home. They knew the punishment for trying to escape was death or even worse. Intimidation played a key role in slavery. In addition, escaped slaves would have to cross many states to the West or to the North to find freedom. They would have little assistance along the way.

On Thursday and Friday of that week, Kelley returned to help out. As had become the norm, I really had nothing for her to do. We just talked and laughed. She would assist me with the simple task of setting up the church and paying the bills. I did not need assistance in that area, but I dared not tell her that. I needed her presence in other ways.

Kelley left to go back home on Friday afternoon. This was an awkward goodbye. I knew that our plan to help the slaves escape could get me in a lot of trouble and I may not be able to see Kelley again. This did not deter me from the mission, but it did concern me a little.

As darkness approached, Earl, Charlotte, and I ate a small dinner. We knew we did not need an overly full belly as our task approached.

"A full belly make you sleepy. You will also be slow in the feet. Don't you boys eat too much. Put that biscuit down, Earl," Charlotte said.

I loved her way. She was always right. A true philosopher with words to live by.

Following dinner, I led us in a prayer. It seemed appropriate to be asking the Lord for guidance, wisdom, and safety. I also asked that we do what is right for all. During times like these,

I always wonder where the line between obeying God's Law and man's law is. The Bible says, "Render unto Caesar what is Caesar's." That could be interpreted two separate ways. First that man should obey man's law as well as God's Law. It could also be interpreted that man should obey God's Law above all else because, in reality, nothing on earth belongs to Caesar.

As a pastor, that is the toughest question to answer, and at the same time the easiest question to answer. We should follow man's law as long as it is consistent with God's Law. If man's law goes against Biblical teaching than we are under no obligation to follow it. The concept of "humanity above civility" or perhaps "divinity over civility" as I deemed it.

Shortly after dark, Charlotte began to get into her disguise. We took moss from the old oak trees to put in her hair. We applied some marsh mud to her face to give it a grayish tint as well. Earl and I took Charlotte around to some of the nearby plantations. We wanted Charlotte to go near some of the slave quarters and even the main plantation houses. We had to make sure she stayed far enough away as to not get caught or be recognized. We simply wanted to establish the presence of the Hag in the area on that night. Many of the Africans as well as the whites saw her in the shadows.

As midnight approached, Earl and I took up our positions. I headed down Rockville Road toward the Davis plantation. I was going to help the children once they neared the road to get toward the church. Earl was stationed near the main intersection adjacent to the old cemetery.

Not too long after arriving, I saw the children coming down the drive of the plantation. I rushed toward them and said, "Do not make a sound. Tonight you will sleep with your mom and dad."

The children, around 4 and 6 years old, respectfully obeyed. They were a little scared but followed me up the road. We ran as fast as we could, and at one point, I had one of them on my back and the other in my arms. I had the strength of three men at that point. As we neared the main intersection, I heard some dogs barking off in the distance from where we had come. I knew it would not take long for them to find the children were missing.

I saw Earl running from the other direction with two adults close behind. At that point we ran on the grassy side of the road so as not to make any more footprints. I guided the united family through the woods past the Slave Boneyard up beside the church. The family entered the Revolutionary War crypt and headed down into the underground chamber. I sealed the door and quickly looked for Earl coming close behind. I did not see him so I quickly backtracked. In the distance, I heard men on horses quickly approaching.

Earl was in the process of spreading the old bones along the side of the road and then he quickly joined me on our way back. Charlotte did her part as well. She was responsible for letting out a wild, screeching cackle. We had to play up the concept that the Hag was around. We all then proceeded quickly to our sleeping quarters and put on our sleeping clothes. I was unsure what would happen next. The slave family was reunited in the secret tunnel, safe and quiet for now. I waited to see if anyone would come near the church to search for the escapees.

All that night we heard the barking of dogs, the clatter of horses, and the loud calls of the slave trackers. "They went this way." "Here they are!" "I see them!" Although I knew the family was safe, I did not sleep very well that night if at all. There is an old saying that both "the bad and the good usually sleep soundly, both content with their day." I guess that put me somewhere in the middle that night.

The next morning, I got out of bed at sunrise. Both Earl and Charlotte were in the kitchen behind the house fixing breakfast. I said, "I hope you both slept well."

Charlotte quipped back, "You have to sleep to sleep well."

"I know what you mean," I replied.

We were all hesitant to actually talk about what we had done or the fact that the slave family was hidden away. We had put enough food there in the tunnel for a few days knowing that we would not be able to check on them. I knew Earl and Charlotte felt we had done the right thing, but they were still visibly uneasy. I too was a little uneasy. I tried to speak some words of encouragement.

"This is the last I am going to say about this today. We did the right thing. We helped people. We helped those kids. We may all end up dead, but I do not want to live with the images of those sad children's faces crying for their parents. Living that way is worse than dying. I would rather die for something than live for nothing. That would be betraying myself and my

Lord," I explained. I was probably trying to convince myself more than the other two that what we had done was right.

Before we could eat any breakfast, a group of men on horses came around led by Mr. Davis's foreman. I did not know his name and did not really care to learn it. He was widely known for being particularly cruel to those he managed.

The man said, "Pastor, we need you to take a look at something."

I followed them down the drive of the church. My heart raced. Did I leave something of mine at the scene of the slave escape? Was there something that made them think that we were involved? It was an arduous walk to the end of the drive. As we proceeded out onto the main road, I saw a scattering of blood-covered bones and tattered clothing all over the place.

"What do you make of this?" I asked.

The foreman said, "Near as we can tell, I think the Hag may have gotten those escaped slaves. A family escaped last night from our place and another down the road. It looks like they all met up here. That hag must have made a meal of the lot of them."

I said with a trembling voice, "It does appear as though they are gone. I hope the Lord is with them now." I really was scared. This was no act.

The foreman said, "I bet they are down below. Them slaves didn't go to heaven."

"You may be right," I agreed. "They very well could be."

He went on, "Well them slaves may be right about that old hag. She does kill people and eat 'em. Clean to the bone. At least this will keep more of them from trying to escape."

"I will have Earl and Charlotte clean this mess and dispose of these bones. They will get to stinkin' if we leave them out here in this hot sun for another day. I will talk to some of the Island's landowners. We will need to figure out what to do about this," I concluded and went back down the drive to the church.

I saw Earl and Charlotte and asked them to clean up the mess out on the main road. I recommended that they bury the bones in the Slave Boneyard. After all, that was where they had originally come from anyway. I encouraged them to do it quickly so those that may know better about what really happened would not scrutinize the scene. We all had to play our roles as if we knew nothing more than the others.

"By the way, the blood was a good idea." I winked at Earl.

It was Saturday afternoon by the time we all had cleaned up all of the remnants of the plan. I had to quickly finalize the plan for the next day's sermon. I would not preach on the Ten Commandments as we had told the parishioners, but I had planned all along to discuss more about spirits, the Hag, and what it meant for all of us. I felt a little silly scaring people like this, but it was necessary. I figured I would try to calm their fears at some level. We did not want an island full of panicked and scared people.

That night I went through the basement door and down the tunnel to check on the slave family. They all looked well. They were scared, dirty, and a little hungry, but somehow all of that did not seem to matter to them. I saw the love in their eyes for one another.

I took a few minutes to give them a bag full of food that Charlotte had prepared. I also gave them a copy of the map that I had drawn of all of the landmarks between here and Richmond. I told them to stay just off the main road, but follow beside it to Richmond. Once there, head due north until they get to freedom.

"It will be a long, hard journey. You may not all make it, but you will be together. Enjoy that time together. Love one another. I wish you well." I finished with a prayer for their safety. I honestly thought that they probably would not all make it to freedom. I hoped that I had not created more problems for this family than I had solved. I hoped I was doing what was best for them and not what was best for my conscience. In life, sometimes all you can do is set the table; folks have to eat for themselves.

"In one hour we will give you a signal. At that time, go through the tunnel and out the crypt door. You are on you way. You will be in our prayers. God will watch over you." I figured that would be the last words I ever spoke to this family.

Once Earl and I checked around the perimeter of the church property, we gave the signal. There was no one out that night. Word of a hag on the loose had spread rapidly throughout the island. Although many people claimed they did not believe in such spirits, they did not want to find out otherwise. Ironically enough, I was not even sure if those hags were real. Evil spirits are all around in many forms. The family headed out that night and we never heard nor saw them again.

The talk on the island for the next few weeks was all about the supposed death of that escaped slave family. The landowners were a little uneasy about what may be wandering about out there in the woods. There was little worry of escape by the island's slaves at that point. The Africans were scared that they may be the next victim. None of them wanted to wander about the island at night. That hag was real for now anyway.

That Sunday, I decided not to give a formal sermon. Instead we talked about what had happened on our island. People wanted to know if the evil spirits were real and if they would really kill people. I could say with all honesty that I believed it was a real possibility that spirits may roam our island and that they were very capable of destroying lives.

Others took a different view of what had happened. This was the evident case for the arrogant, self-righteous nature of many slave owners. They would say, "Those slaves were killed by those spirits because they were trying to escape. That was God's way of punishing them for being disobedient."

Obviously nothing could have been farther from reality, but I did not go out of my way to dispel this view because it worked to our advantage. The last thing I wanted was for people to believe that those slaves were alive and on the run. And equally important, I did not want people to know that I had helped them escape.

That Sunday night was the first chance I had to collect my thoughts. The events of the last few days had been invigorating. I felt like I was finally doing some good. Doing good deeds can many times be like an addiction. You constantly need to keep doing those things that bring pleasure to you. I knew I wanted to help more of the Africans, but I had to wait for the appropriate time. It may be months or years, but I knew I would do it again. My goal in the interim was to direct my sermons toward the hearts of those on the island. I needed to begin to try to change them on the inside. The phrase "Love one another" was a constant echo in my soul.

CONSE-QUENCES

THE NEXT FEW MONTHS were somewhat uneventful. Kelley still came around the church two or three days a week. Both of us wanted to see each other more, but we knew it would not look right if we spent too much time alone. The people of the island may think we were courting.

The feel of autumn was in the air. Personally it was my favorite time of the year on Johns Island. The summers in this part of the country tend to be long, hot, and humid. Fall brings a cool, crisp feeling to the air. It always seems to rejuvenate everyone's spirit around here.

It is also one of my favorite times to live near the tidal creeks of Johns Island. There is an abundance of activity in the tidal marsh and a lot of good things to eat. Shrimp and crabs are abundant in autumn. The shrimp come in to the creeks to lay their eggs. Earl and I went out many a day with a seine net. We would pull in 20 or 30 pounds of shrimp and crabs. We ate most of them and shared some with others. The Africans on the island knew of a lot of unique ways to prepare fishes and shellfishes. We always ate well this time of year.

In addition to the fruits of the sea, there were also many crops that produced well in the fall. Yams and greens were two of my favorites. I always loved a dinner of yams, greens, and cornbread or Johnnycake. A favorite dessert this time of year was pear crisp. Pears grew fairly well down here although we never had much luck growing other fruits such as apples.

One day in late September, Kelley came to help us. She had requested that she and I go on one of our picnics down by the tidal creek. I, of course, obliged. We spread a blanket and ate some snacks. I brought along a fishing line to see if we could catch a trout or flounder, both of which were good to eat and fun to catch. I always said that I would never marry a woman that did not like to fish. Luckily Kelley liked to. I probably would have made an exception for her.

As we sat there in the cool autumn air, I sensed that something was bothering Kelley. She did not seem mad, but uneasy. Kind of like the feeling you get when you need to tell someone something unpleasant, but you are waiting for the right time.

Kelley pulled out a doll from her basket and held it out in front of me. She did not speak a word. I froze with fear but did my best to hide my concern.

She said, "Do you know whose this is?"

"I don't recognize it right off hand," I replied. I knew exactly whose that was. It was the doll of that little slave girl whose family we had helped to escape. I had no idea where this conversation would lead so I did not offer any additional information.

Kelley said, "Do you know where I found it?"

Again I played ignorant. "Well, of course not. I do not even know whose it is." It was very awkward to lie to Kelley. I did not like the way it made me feel. Again it conjured up that age-old question that had constantly gnawed at me. Was it all right to lie a little to accomplish a greater good? I wasn't sure if I would ever be able to answer that question completely.

Kelley began to speak quietly but directly. "Yesterday while working in the basement of the church, I found a secret passage behind the closet wall. I followed it to find a small room and another passage that led to the old Revolutionary War crypt. In that small underground room, I found this doll. This doll belonged to that little slave girl who we saw being separated from her mother in Charleston. I will never forget that image. Would you like to tell me about how it may have gotten there?"

At this point, I did not know how to proceed. I was not sure if Kelley thought that I may be involved with the death of those slaves as most people believed was their fate or if I may have helped them to escape. Neither position is held in that high esteem in Southern culture during this day.

I looked Kelley in the eye and I broke down in tears. "I cannot lie to you. You are my one true love. I was meant to be with you forever. I will tell you the truth, every detail. I will let you do what you will with the facts."

I recapped my life over the last few months since my epiphany at Seminary and all the events since. I summarized my plan to help reunite the slave family and help them escape. I made clear that Earl and Charlotte were just following my orders. None of this was their idea. The last thing I wanted was to get them in trouble.

Kelley looked down and said, "Josiah, you too were the love of my life. I never knew I could care for someone this deeply. But you have broken the law. I do not like everything about slavery but it is the way in this land. You cannot go around and take things from people and stir up mischief. The whole island has been scared to go out after dark. What kind of man are you? What kind of pastor are you?"

Kelley stood up with tears in her eyes and walked back toward the church. She climbed up onto the wagon and instructed the driver to take her home. I did not know what she would do with the information I had told her. Would she tell her father? Would I ever see her or touch her hand again?

This was the reward for my good deed. I still knew that what I had done was right but it did not feel so right then.

That night, over dinner, I had to tell Earl and Charlotte what had happened with Kelley that day. They both were somewhat scared but resigned to the fact that we would probably all be killed if Kelley told anyone.

Earl said, "I figured we would be found out one day. I'd rather go be free in heaven than watch all this down here."

My life at that moment became difficult, to say the least. I did not know what would happen. Not only did I face potential imprisonment or death, I also faced the reality of knowing that I would be responsible if Earl or Charlotte were killed as well.

I also had just lost the one true love of my life. Many people claim to fall in love multiple times, but people typically only have one true love. As if all of that was not enough, I also had to face the fact that my position as a pastor may be in jeopardy even if the whole truth were not disclosed.

My deepest hope was that Kelley would value what we had enough to simply keep silent. I knew I had lost her forever, but maybe I could maintain my existence here.

The next day while we were working out in the cemetery near the church, a carriage approached being driven by Mr. Prose. I figured my time of reckoning was here. He stopped alongside us and said, "I hear you all have been pretty busy lately."

"Well, uh, yes sir," I replied. I did not know what he meant by the question, but I did not want to volunteer anything.

He went on, "Kelley has told me about all of the chores you all have completed and that you said you would not need her to come around any more. She was quite upset you know."

"I do apologize for upsetting her. She is a fine young lady and I would never do anything to hurt her. We just have things pretty much in order around here. I did not want to keep her from her other pursuits and interests. She is welcome to stop by any time," I said, hoping that was all that Kelley had told her father. "Earl and Charlotte have been most helpful. I would appreciate it if they could stay on around here. I would be willing to pay you for their labor."

"You keep them. It is my contribution to the church," Mr. Prose said.

It seemed strange to talk about Earl and Charlotte like property, but such was the way.

Mr. Prose left. His presence reminded me of how much I would miss Kelley. I was, however, relieved that she had not told her father the truth about the escaped slaves. I knew I would always live in fear of what we had done. I also knew that I wanted to help more slaves. That would be my mission. I would have to fill the emptiness created by Kelley's departure with other activities.

I planned to begin a sermon series on love. Initially I had planned to do these sermons to help change the hearts of the people of the island. To make them rethink slavery without coming right out and saying that. I still had that in mind, but having tasted love with Kelley, these sermons had additional meaning.

Love is a very complex word to define. It has countless meanings and many connotations. It can mean a longing, a passion, a lust, or a necessity for something or someone. A man once said, "Love is like quicksand; you can't see it until you are in it." As simplistic as that sounds, it is accurate. Whether it is the love of God or of another human, you cannot really describe love, but you know it when you feel it.

I decided to depart from my home and head down toward the seashore. I planned to go toward Seabrook Island, a mostly uninhabited stretch of land sandwiched between several large marsh inlets and the great Atlantic Ocean. There were several secluded areas down there where I had hoped to collect my thoughts and refocus on my life.

As I arrived at a small grove of trees overlooking the tidal creeks, I could see Rockville in the distance. It had long been a fishing and shrimping village that fed much of these islands. The beauty was overwhelming, but I was a bit saddened. It is difficult to be a man in this society with troubles. A man with pain in your heart. Our role is to be the strong rock for others to lean upon. A man was to be a sturdy oak that the children climb upon and the wife swings upon. Currently I was none of that.

My emotions were further challenged by the fact that I was a pastor. We are not supposed to get caught up in the emotions of the world. We should know that all things are God's plan and all will work out in the end. At least that is the perception that others have of pastors. In reality, no one is promised a simple life here on earth. There is no scripture that says if you have a certain profession or if you behave a certain way that your life will be easy. In fact, life is typically more difficult for those who try to live a good life. There is so much more to turn away from. It is much easier in the South today to support slavery and own slaves than to oppose it and want to set them free.

I also began to understand my father a little more deeply. He was always a quiet, introspective man. I see now why that may have been the case. He lost his only daughter, my sister, at age 5 to a grave illness. What was he to do with all of that anger and grief? He kept it inside. He probably felt like I felt right then. I was afraid to start crying for fear I may never stop.

I resigned myself to the fact that I may always carry an eternal sadness, but I could not let that be an excuse to avoid helping others. My burden did not belong to others. I must move on. I must continue my mission. Until all the slaves were free, I would have a mission. I knew that the chances of living to see the end of slavery were doubtful, but I would soldier on. Passion is the anticipation of attainment.

I utilized the time on Seabrook Island to craft a few sermons. I needed to redirect my life and others' to focus on love. Love of one another. That would be the only way to achieve independence for all. I pulled a lot of stories and quotes from the Bible about love and dispersed them throughout my sermons. Again, I kept coming back to that simple quote, "Love one another." Jesus really need not say more.

On my way home, I began to think about a more practical approach to the anti-slavery mission. I would write a book, probably under another name, outlining the Bible's depiction of slavery. A few things always stand out in Biblical stories of slavery. First, God always set His people free when they were enslaved. Never immediately, but always. Second, although there are stories about bondmen obeying their masters, God never condoned the unjust and ill treatment of another human.

I would one day convey these principles to others. For a book perhaps entitled *The Biblical Companion on Slavery and Race Relations* I began to jot down notes on that very night.

As Thanksgiving approached, we planned a big gathering on the church grounds. All of the parishioners were invited to come and bring food to share. Thanksgiving was one of the best holidays around here. It was very family-oriented and we all were thankful for what we had. Thankful to God and to those around us. Earl, Charlotte, and I were thankful that no one had found us out.

On that day, we had a great time. The children were playing games and running all about the church. The adults were eating some great food and catching up on current events. There was little to no talk about the escaped slaves. One person did mention that the Hag must have moved on since there had been no sightings lately. The conversation quickly changed to other topics, which gave me some relief.

Mr. and Mrs. Prose did attend, but they said that Kelley was not feeling well and chose to stay back at the plantation. I hoped that this was true. I did not hope that she was sick, but I did hope that there was a reason she stayed home other than a desire to avoid seeing me.

I must say that Thanksgiving Day was the first day that I remembered feeling something other than deep sadness since the day Kelley walked away from my life. I would still see her in the congregation while I was preaching, but she would leave soon after the service with her family. We had exchanged a few polite words here and there, but it was clear that I had hurt her beyond repair. Hopefully, time would heal that wound. I was not expecting her to ever love me again; I just did not want her to hate me forever.

I realized that I needed to seek some advice from someone that I respected who may understand the situation that I was in. I planned a trip back up to Richmond to seek counsel from Pastor Simon. He was my mentor back in Seminary and motivated me to think deeper about the spiritual aspects of slavery.

He does not know to what extent I took those deeper thoughts, but he inspired me to do more.

This was somewhat of an impromptu trip, but I would be able to travel on Monday and return on Saturday so I would not miss my Sunday duties. The steam train was running consistently now between Charleston and several other cities. It would be fairly easy to make it to Richmond in a day or two.

I boarded the train on the Monday after Thanksgiving. A train is an interesting place to see a sampling of the world. You have people from all walks of life. Some people are going to somewhere. Others are escaping from somewhere. It gives you a chance to take stock of your own life. I was seated in a passenger car with what looked like a newlywed couple. It stung a little to see others enjoying the love that I had lost, but I tried to be happy for them. This was the Christian thing to do. It is easy to be happy for others when you are happy. It is much more difficult when you are not. That is the true measure of one's faith.

I arrived in Richmond early on Tuesday morning. I headed straight over to the Seminary. Pastor Simon was teaching a class when I arrived. I quietly walked into the room and sat at the back of the class. Pastor Simon instantly acknowledged me with a nod of the head, but went on teaching. I had hoped to remain quiet in the back of the class until he was finished. The subject of the lecture was the Ten Commandments. Following the robust discussion, the class was dismissed. I approached the podium and greeted Pastor Simon with a hug.

"What brings you all the way here from Charleston, Pastor Whitby?" he asked. "It must be an issue about love or morality. That always brings you new pastors back."

"I have come to seek your wisdom and counsel on many of life's great issues," I responded with a slight grin. This was only a slight exaggeration.

We proceeded to the pastor's office where he closed the door. I think he could tell by my unexpected arrival as well as my solemn demeanor that I needed some help.

"Do you remember the lecture you gave during the last week of school? The one on Jesus' greatest commandment to love one another," I began. "I had inquired if the slave was included in the 'one another.' The class proceeded to have a rather robust discussion on the issue of slavery. I have not been able to get past that issue. I feel that the Africans are God's children as well and we have no right to treat them inhumanely. Am I wrong?"

Pastor Simon leaned his chair back and pulled his spectacles off, and then he replied, "Are you wrong? Well that depends on who you ask. If you walk down the street here in Richmond or in Charleston, most people would say that you were wrong. That is the beauty of the Bible and God's Word though; it is not subject to the whims of society or the passing fads of fashion."

He sipped a bit of tea before going on. "I can find no place in the Bible where God refuses to call someone His child as long as they believe in Jesus. You will not find the phrase "except Africans" or "except slaves" anywhere in the Bible. Many people would like to believe that God does not like a certain group, but that is not the case. So the answer to your question is that you are right. Slavery is wrong as practiced most places," Pastor Simon concluded. "So what are we to do about that?"

"I am not sure what to do, but I know I need to do something," I replied. I had no interest in telling Pastor Simon about some of the things I had done to help slaves escape. I just needed to make sure that I was thinking clearly on these issues. I actually think the good pastor would have helped me on my mission had I asked.

We had dinner that night at a local restaurant and reminisced about the 5 years that I had spent at the Seminary. Pastor Simon had taught there for 30 years so he had seen many a young pastor charge out of school with a mission only to be pulled back down to earth by all of the worldly forces. At the end of our dinner, the Pastor walked me back to my hotel.

"You be careful, Josiah Whitby. Your passion must be tempered with good judgment. God created the world in 6 days. Do you really think you can perfect the world as quickly? Be patient. Right will win. One way or the other it always does." With that, Pastor Simon departed.

I returned to the Richmond Inn to settle for the night. I turned in around 10:00 p.m. I had planned to head back to Charleston in two days, but I wanted to see more of Richmond before leaving. My slumber was interrupted by the screams of a woman in a room nearby to my own. After putting on my pants, I entered the hallway to find a group of white men dragging one of the hotel's black servants away. The young lady was screaming. "He came in my room while I was dressing! I don't know what he would have done to me!"

Unable to mind my own business, I followed the mob down the stairs to the back of the inn. One of the proprietors of the establishment strung up the servant on two poles. His arms were outstretched and his clothes were torn off. He was beaten with a whip. I turned away, not able to bear the vision of his pain. Following the spectacle, the crowd dispersed. I walked quietly over to the slave who had been cut loose to lie on the ground. Since I was a pastor, no one made a big deal of the fact that I approached someone in need even if he was a slave.

"Are you alright?" I asked.

"I be alright soon enough. This ain't the first time this happens," the man replied.

"What is your name?" I continued.

"Jacob," he muttered, almost out of breath.

"Tell me what happened. Did you aim to harm that young lady?" I inquired.

"No, sir. I works here and she had ordered some food to be delivered to her room. I knocked on the door and it came open. She was standing there half dressed. I did not really even look at her. I turned away. She starts a screaming about how I am gonna get her," the African man said.

This was many times the case in our world. There was a deep sensitivity to the Africans looking at or being attracted to the white women. It was all overblown. In reality, it was the white slave owners who took liberties with the African slaves. You see all shades of the African rainbow in the South.

I told Jacob to get himself healed. I would need his help in transporting my bags to the train station in two days. I planned to buy some goods to transport back to Charleston with me. I looked him clear in the eye and said, "If you want to be free, that will be your day to run. If not, I will seek others who never want to be wrongly accused again."

As usual, I had no formal plan, but I was going to do something. Upon waking the next morning, I went around Richmond to see what had changed in the year or so since I had left. It was still a lovely city with many historic sites. The grandeur of the old houses was not at all unlike my beloved city. My final stop of the day was at one of the larger mercantile shops. I purchased a large trunk to help transport some goods back home.

That night I ordered some food to be delivered to my room. I knew that Jacob was working until midnight that night, so I planned to discuss the following day's agenda with him. I told him to come to my room before daybreak the next day with anything he wanted to take with him. He was very interested in the chance to escape to anywhere that he could live free. It was almost impossible for slaves to escape without the help of whites since there was such a heightened level of suspicion.

I really did not sleep at all that night. As always, the excitement or fear of helping a slave escape overwhelmed me. I could not relax enough to rest. Jacob knocked on my door around 5:00 a.m. I promptly let him in. I gave him one of my suits to put on so he would not look like an escaped servant. Just before sunrise, I locked him in the large trunk and called for one of the servants that was currently on duty to help me carry my bags down to the inn's carriage. The carriage would take me to the train station.

A fairly young African boy, probably around 13, arrived at my door to carry my bags. I had not planned on this. He would not be strong enough to carry the trunk. I told him to grab one end and I would get the other. We managed to drag the heavy trunk down the steps, knocking against a few spindles along the way.

The proprietor came out from his office to inquire about the noise. "What in the world do you have in there, Pastor, a dead body?"

I smiled nervously and came back with, "No, a live body." I then laughed rather loudly to make him think I was kidding. I then said, "I am doing the Lord's work. The contents of this trunk will help me to help others. The Bible is a heavy book you know." Those few comments bought me enough time to load the trunk on the carriage and head toward the train station.

Upon arrival at the station, I asked to assist in loading the trunk onto the baggage car. I was insistent that nothing be placed on top of the trunk since it was "possessions of the Lord" that I was transporting that could not risk damage. The plan was for me to unlock the trunk and leave it that way. Jacob was to open the trunk while en route. He was then free to depart the train and head North on his own.

As was the case with the other slaves I had helped, I felt like I was leaving a lot up to God. I would help them escape their owners, but I never saw them achieve freedom up North or out West. I guess I was doing the best I could at that time. I told myself that anyway so I did not feel guilty.

Upon arrival in Charleston, I proceeded to the baggage car to pick up the trunk. It was very light now. I could carry it all by myself. I put my other bags inside and met Earl outside the station. We proceeded back to the church grounds to get back to the daily activities. The holiday season was approaching, which meant that there would be more church functions in the next month. I looked forward to the distractions. My mind was still a bit shaken and my heart a bit lonesome. Kelley being the cause for the latter.

CHRISTMAS

As December began, our minds turned to Christmas. It was a very exciting time for everyone on Johns Island. The children in the church began their weekly practice for the annual Christmas play. I had always enjoyed the performance ever since I was young and participated myself. Now I was in charge. It was quite a challenge to help 25 children learn their parts and for me to direct the action. Charlotte was kind enough to help fix the old costumes and make a few new ones.

One day over lunch, I began to discuss Christmas with Earl and Charlotte. I asked them if they had ever heard the legend of St. Nicholas. The famed story of a Saint in Europe hundreds of years ago that would go around giving gifts to children on Christmas Eve. They both were somewhat familiar with the story since many of the residents on Johns Island still practiced this tradition of giving their children gifts in the night and pretending that they were left by St. Nicholas.

I asked them, "Do any of the slave children ever get gifts on Christmas Eve?"

"No slave has much to give their childrens. All they got is what the master gives them," Earl said.

"Well this year, Earl, we are going to change that," I said, having just hatched my next plan. I was going to be St. Nicholas, or St. Josiah. I was going to go around at night on Christmas Eve and give all of the slave children a small gift and maybe some candy.

Earl and Charlotte laughed out loud. "Mister Josiah, you are just plain crazy. I think you want to get caught helping us slaves," Charlotte said.

"I will tell both of you the same thing I told you last time: you do not have to help me one bit if you do not want to. I will never ask either of you to take any risks that are too great for your comfort," I said. "But I must admit I like working with you on these things. It's fun to help people with people you like."

"We are in this deep at this point. We are going to ride this horse until it stops. It may run into the ocean. It may run into a tree. Or, it may just stop on its own and we fly over the front. But we are gonna ride on," Earl said.

I must admit, I felt relieved. Maybe a bit empowered by their assistance.

Charlotte volunteered to make some little dolls out of sweetgrass. She made several each day. It would take a while to make enough for all of the little African girls on the island. Earl and I made some toys out of wood for the boys. I planned to make a trip into Charleston to buy some additional toys and candy. Thank goodness Charleston was far enough away that I could buy toys there without raising a lot of suspicion.

I read some old books about St. Nicholas. I wanted to be authentic in my approach. In some countries the secular aspects of Christmas had begun to overshadow the real meaning. I in no way wanted that to happen around here. I was planning to give these children a gift just as God had given the world a gift on that first Christmas long ago.

My research on Santa Claus was quite interesting. St. Nicholas was born in the city of Myra about 300 years before the birth of Jesus. He was orphaned while still young. Both of his parents died from the plague. Nicholas grew up in a monastery and became one of the youngest priests ever at age 17. Later Nicholas went on to become a bishop, which is why many of the early depictions show him in a bishop's robe and hat. St. Nicholas was known to travel about the countryside giving gifts to the poor and less fortunate, especially children. He would often drop bags of gold down chimneys.

The Reformation of the Catholic Church led the Protestants to modify their view of the gift-giving patron. He began to be viewed less as a Catholic Bishop and more like a grandfatherly figure. The Dutch were some of the first immigrants to bring this jolly gift-giver to America. They called him Sinterklaas. Most children in America mispronounced this, giving us his current name of Santa Claus.

The current view of Santa Claus was most fervently established by the classic writings of Washington Irving and later by Clement Moore. Dr. Moore's poem entitled "A Visit from St.

Nicholas" had become a traditional Christmas story all over the country. Many of the slave children were aware of the story, it having been passed down orally through the generations.

Christmas in America was still, as it should be, a religious celebration of Jesus' birth. But many of the traditions used for this celebration in other countries had arrived here as well. The Scandinavians introduced the folklore of gift-giving elves. The Germans decorated evergreen trees as a symbol of eternal life and the Irish gave us a tradition of putting candles in the windows during the Christmas season.

I was also in the process of planning my Christmas Eve service. That would be the night that the children performed their Christmas play about the birth of Jesus and I would give a brief sermon on the importance of that day. I began to get more and more excited as Christmas Eve approached. I was never sure what motivated me those days. Was it the thought of helping others or the thought of doing something secretly? I hoped in my mind that I was doing what God wanted me to do. Occasionally, a deed can begin as a Godly mission but evolve into a selfish obsession. Those carrying out God's work are not God. The hand is not the body, but a tool of the body.

On that Christmas Eve, the majority of the island's residents came to the church. It was always funny to me that people felt obligated to come to church on Easter and Christmas. They were standing in the aisles on those days. The children's play went off as expected. There were the usual forgotten lines and wardrobe issues, but overall it was a great joy to see the kids acting out the first Christmas.

I had the somewhat challenging job of following the play with my sermon. Pastor Phillips had always tried to keep the Christmas Eve service short so folks could get home and celebrate. Many people would put up an evergreen tree and decorate it as a part of their Christmas activities. The evergreen was becoming a symbol of Jesus at Christmas time.

On that night, Kelley and her family sat right near the front. I could not take my eyes off of her during the play. Every time I saw her it was both painful and joyful. As long as I knew she was still out there and unwed, I felt that I may have a chance to regain her love. The painful part was that I did not think she could ever trust or respect me again. If she could not, we would never have a future.

I concluded the sermon with a prayer. ". . . Just as Jesus was sent to earth to forgive us for our sins, let us forgive the sins of others. Let us all pass on the free gift that was given to us. Amen."

As I opened my eyes at the end of the prayer, Kelley was staring directly at me. She turned away quickly with a tear welling in her eye. I think deep down she wanted to give me another chance. Once you taste heartbreak, you typically spend the rest of your life trying to avoid it.

The congregation arose from their seats and made their way home. It was an exceptionally cold night in the low-country of South Carolina and clouds obscured the moonlight. It was not a good night to travel around, but it was a good night for Santa Claus, also known tonight as Santa Josiah, to sneak about and leave gifts.

Following a nice dinner (it always seems like every major event in the South is either preceded or followed by a nice dinner), I began to collect the toys in an old sack. Earl and I were not sure what the best way was to transport all of the gifts around the island before sunrise without making too much noise. We chose to put the items on the carriage and use the horses to pull us around. We did not take the time to think up an alibi if we were to be confronted by the islanders. Again an example of my poor planning that I had come to refer to as blind faith.

Earl and I proceeded to the south end of the island first. We would work our way back to the north and east. I intentionally wanted to visit the Prose plantation last. The evening was fairly uneventful. Earl would stop the carriage near the main road and I would jump out with a sack full of toys. I had to sneak through the woods or walk in the shadow of the main drive to get to the slave quarters. Most everyone was asleep. A few children awoke as I laid a toy in their arms or alongside their bed. I left a few pieces of candy as well.

I must admit it was quite a joyful experience. To do nice things for others when they are not expecting it. It also seemed like such a small gesture. These people were enslaved. They were property. They had to work long hours with no pay. They were beaten and in some cases their own children were taken from them. All I was doing was giving them some small gift. Nonetheless, I hoped the small gift would bring them some joy.

Lastly, we were at the Prose plantation. I told Earl to take the carriage on home as I carried the last sack of toys to deliver to the African children. I quietly delivered a toy to each of the slave quarters. There was just one sweetgrass doll and a stick of candy left.

I had a plan for these gifts. I climbed up a tree adjacent to Kelley's window and climbed quietly inside. When I wasn't acting crazy helping the slaves, I was acting crazy out of love for Kelley. I put the gifts beside her bed with a little note:

"Please forgive me. I promise I will never mislead you again. St. Nicholas."

I sneaked back out the window and down the tree. I broke a small branch and fell a few feet to the ground. I jumped up and ran for the cover of the woods as quickly as possible. I would surely end my career as a minister if I were caught sneaking out of a young lady's bedroom at night.

During my long walk back home, a few snow flurries began to fall. This was unusual for Charleston. We only get snow about once every 10 years. This was the year, I guess. Interestingly, I liked the snow. I had experienced it quite often while at Seminary.

I slept well that night. It was a peaceful feeling to know that I had asked for forgiveness from Kelley. In addition, Christmas Eve was always a night that was special to me. I looked forward to seeing my family the next day and feasting on a grand meal. We would also exchange some small gifts with each other. The Africans were even given the day off, which made the day feel even more special.

That Christmas day came and went like a blur. It was always that way. You look forward to all the fun activities. It is a day when we put many of our petty differences aside and enjoy each other's company. I returned to my house that evening feeling satisfied. I lay down to sleep. My slumber was soon interrupted.

"Josiah, Josiah," a voice called me as I felt a hand gently shaking me.

I awoke in a foggy mindset to find Kelley above me. She was in tears. She could hardly speak.

"Josiah, they beat him and beat her. They almost killed them. They just kept whipping them and hitting them. There was blood everywhere. I didn't know what to do," Kelley managed to say.

"Slow down," I said. "Tell me what happened."

Kelley explained the events of that Christmas night and day. "We awoke on Christmas morning to find many of the slave children excited and dancing around. They had been given gifts. They were having so much fun. I heard one of them say 'Santa Claus must love us too. He brought us a toy.' I was watching them play from my window and it gave me great pleasure.

"The peace of Christmas afternoon was shattered by chaos. Guilford, one of my father's slave supervisors, was yelling at all of the slave children. He was collecting all of the toys and putting them in a bag. He said, 'None of you will have any of these toys. You all are just lucky you are alive and that we feed you. Be glad that you have the day off.' He went on to say, 'I am going to find out which one of you stirred up all of this trouble and when I do, you will regret it.'

"Apparently Guilford had some reason to suspect that Jed, one of the older slave men and husband of my nanny, Miss Pearl, was responsible for the toys. Jed is a carpenter. Most of the toys were made of wood, so they went after Jed. It was awful. Jed was strung up against a tree and beaten with a whip as well as sticks. It was too much to watch. I knew Jed was innocent, but there was nothing I could do to help. After they beat Jed, they went on to beat Pearl. I guess they thought she was in on it as well."

"I am responsible for this," I lamented. "It is my fault that Jed and Pearl had to suffer. I knew I should have thought things through." I was really distraught. "I was trying to do good, but instead brought evil. I am not the man I try to be."

Kelley slowly continued, ". . . I also received a gift from Santa Claus." She gave a sad smile. "And the letter that accompanied the gift looked dramatically like your handwriting. Josiah, this is not your fault," she said. "No one should be beaten for trying to make a child happy. This is Guilford's fault. And more importantly, it is slavery's fault. I now see why you helped that family. I now see why you want to help the Africans. I want to help you. I want to be your partner." Tears streamed down her face. She looked me right in the eye and said, "I want to be your wife."

The world stopped. I looked back at her. "I want you with all of my soul. I want you to be my wife. I want to be your husband. I will lay down my life for you. I want you to be proud of me. I will strive to make you smile every day. I love you now and forever."

We kissed. Our first kiss. It was magical. It was spiritual. I must admit that finding love on earth makes my faith make more sense.

I told Kelley I would take her back to her house in my carriage. She had run all this way in the dark. I must admit I did not want her to leave, but I would certainly never violate her faith in me. I took my faith very seriously. We would wait until we were wed to know each other at that level.

I was forgiven. It seemed appropriate to be forgiven on this night. That Christmas night was the best of my life. I had my one true earthly love back with me. I felt as though I could do anything. Kelley and I discussed our future. We agreed that we would not tell her parents just yet about our relationship and desire for marriage. I would have to formally approach her father to ask for her hand. We both were confident that this would not be an issue unless her father was still insistent that she marry a wealthy landowner.

We also discussed my life's other passion, helping the slaves. Kelley said, "We are going to help Jed and Pearl. We have to. I want them to be free. Them and their whole family."

I agreed. In light of the fact that I felt responsible for Jed's and Pearl's beatings and possible deaths, I had to help them. I told Kelley that we would have to make a plan to help them.

I stopped the carriage just outside the gates of the Prose plantation. I gave her another kiss. I knew that I would be able to kiss those lips forever. That was a nice feeling. I helped her out of the carriage and walked her toward the house. I could not take the carriage any closer because I did not want her parents to see me dropping Kelley off. It never looked good for a single man and woman to be together after dark. And the fact that I was a pastor added to the importance of maintaining a moral outward appearance.

After Kelley disappeared inside, I walked silently over to the slave quarters. I found the shack that Jed and Miss Pearl were laid up in. Thankfully they were alone. I entered quietly. They both were a bit startled to see someone coming into their cabin, especially a white man. Once they recognized me, they calmed a bit. I assured them that I meant no harm; I was only there to check on them.

"I am sorry this happened to you both. The evil in this land will one day end. Bless you," I said. I wanted to apologize for my part in their whole ordeal, but I knew the risks were great. Many a slave had turned against other slaves as well as whites to gain favor in the eyes of their master. This led to a significant number of hangings. I left them and returned home with an even deeper sense that I owed both of them something more.

FORGIVE-NESS

I AWOKE THE DAY AFTER Christmas with a feeling that my life had begun anew. A man who experiences unconditional love from a woman feels like he is all-powerful. He feels like he can change the world. It is a misconception that men do not need the love of a woman. You will never find a truly happy man that does not have a great relationship with a woman, most often his wife. One's life is made up of several components: social, spiritual, and intimacy. One cannot be completely content or happy unless all three aspects are fulfilled.

I sent word to Mr. Prose that I would like Kelley to return and help out at the church. There were many things that needed to be done in the late winter and early spring. In reality, I just wanted her there and this time she wanted to be there as well. We needed to plan our future as well as make plans to help others.

Kelley began to come around regularly again. Things were so much better now. I had not realized how heavily my secret life had weighed on me. Now that Kelley knew what I had done and what I wanted to do, I felt emancipated. I was free to think bigger. To do more for more people.

There was a small issue still looming though. I needed to approach Kelley's father to ask for his permission to marry her. While I thought that he liked me, I am sure that he never considered me as a potential son-in-law. Most wealthy landowners, like Mr. Prose, wanted their children to marry into other wealthy families. This was the type of aristocratic inbreeding that gives you institutions such as slavery. The sense of entitlement and that feeling that anything you do is right simply because you do it.

It is the reason that many wealthy people have difficulty knowing God at a deeper level. Most truly religious people develop a core set of beliefs and values and judge their own and others' behaviors based on those beliefs. In other words, their beliefs dictate their actions. Many of those with wealth believe that they can behave any way they wish and others must accept it. Their behavior can be summed up more simply. Their actions dictate their beliefs.

I am by no means against wealth or the acquisition of it. In fact, wealth and competition are what make people work harder and strive to be better. They lead to better products and better processes. They improve all of our lives. I just wish people would behave the same after they acquire great riches as they did before that occurred.

Early in the month of January, Kelley arranged a dinner at her house for both of her parents and us together. I planned to formally ask Mr. Prose for Kelley's hand following the dinner. The meal was quite nice, but I was so nervous I could hardly eat. I was so confident in many aspects of my life. I had a great knowledge of God, I spoke in front of a large group of people every week, and I even was so bold as to break the law to help others, but I was a wreck.

Following the dinner, Mr. Prose asked me to join him in his study. It was customary for the men to congregate after a dinner in a parlor or study to discuss politics, farming, or other events of the day. I was flattered that he considered me a peer at some level. I hoped that after that night he would still like me. At some level, I just hoped to survive that night.

The subject of slavery came up before I had an opportunity to even discuss marriage.

"Josiah, there is talk all over the South that one day the politicians in Washington will try to abolish slavery. I, like most others, do not like slavery in its current form," Mr. Prose said.

Almost every wealthy Southerner would say the same thing when discussing slavery. It was their way of justifying their mistreatment of others. They would always say something to the effect of "I don't like it, but it is the hand we were dealt" or "It is a service to the Africans; they are unable to fend for themselves" or "We would all starve if slavery were abolished; we would be poor and penniless." This was the classic example of behaving badly then creating a value system that justified that bad behavior.

I sat quietly and let Mr. Prose continue. I was in no position to be confrontational at this time. I did plan to let my views be known in a subtle way, but this was not the time to be bold. I needed to continue to work behind the scenes and I needed my partner Kelley by my side.

Mr. Prose went on, "The South may be forced to make some hard decisions one day. We will not be told by those who live up North how to live our life. I will die for what I believe."

"Sir," I replied, "I agree with you at some level. I am a true Southerner at heart. I will not let our way of life die. I do, however, recognize that slavery will not be around forever in the South and we should plan for that eventuality."

I felt like this was a fair answer that did not betray my beliefs but did not raise any controversy either. Again, I knew that being anti-slavery in a public manner would never help my cause.

"I like the way you think, Josiah," Mr. Prose said. "You are a wise young man."

That seemed like my opening to discuss other issues. More important issues, such as my interest in marrying his daughter and becoming the father of his grandchildren. I figured I would not discuss grandchildren, however. Most fathers really do not want to discuss that with their future son-in-law. Can't say as I blame them on that one.

"Mr. Prose, there is a more important issue that I would like to discuss with you this evening. It concerns your daughter. I am in love with her. I think she is the one person in this whole world that was meant for me. I want to marry her. If you will give me your blessing, I plan to do just that. I will promise to take care of her, love her, and provide for her as long as I live," I said with a great amount of confidence.

Mr. Prose simply stared at me for a few moments. It was probably only ten seconds but it felt like a month or more. He was clearly pondering what I had said. He managed to collect his thoughts and respond. "Hmm, I had not really thought too much about my precious Kelley marrying a preacher. Let me study on that for a moment," he said as he lit a cigar.

Then he asked me a string of questions: "Have you discussed this with Kelley? Where would you live? Can you provide for her on your pastor's income?" and so on. I managed to answer the barrage of questions to his satisfaction.

He then conceded with a laugh, "I reckon my Kelley could do a lot worse. I will support the marriage." That was not the ringing endorsement that I had hoped for, but he did give his approval, which was all that I was looking for.

Mr. Prose then said, "You know I always pictured my son-in-law to be a banker or doctor but I think you will be fine."

I responded back, "That's alright, I always pictured my father-in-law to be a lot more handsome. We all make sacrifices." I quickly followed that up with a laugh and a smile to let him know I was joking. I did want to let him know that I could play the game too. I tried to redirect the conversation, having felt that I may have overstepped my bounds.

I thanked Mr. Prose for his approval and vowed again that I would always care for his daughter. I asked Mr. Prose not to say anything yet about our potential engagement, as I wanted to ask Kelley the right way. I wanted to plan something special.

We rejoined the ladies on the front porch of the house, a stately Southern front porch with large columns. I do not consider myself an envious man, but I was quite fond of Kelley's house. I think Kelley was relieved to see me return in one piece. She knew as well as anyone how tough her father could be. She did not know the exact nature of our conversation, but she knew her father would challenge me. As far as Kelley knew, I was simply asking her father for permission to formally court her.

I departed shortly thereafter. I climbed on my carriage and headed back down the dark drive toward the main road. I could not help but think about the Hag. This was the location of the original hag sighting by Charlotte during the Prose gathering. I still was a little unsure if the Hag was real. I knew I did not want to find out. I rode home slightly faster than usual. I did arrive home safely to the church grounds and promptly went to bed.

I asked Kelley to come by the church on that Friday. I needed her help to go into Charleston for supplies. She graciously agreed to help me. I really did need some things from Charleston, but more importantly, I wanted to ask her to marry me. I could not think of a finer location than downtown Charleston.

She arrived that morning looking lovely as ever. She was accompanied by her driver as well as Miss Bessie, her childhood nanny. Miss Bessie was currently Kelley's attendant and in most regards her best friend. I was very fearful that they would want to accompany us into Charleston, but thankfully

Kelley asked them to stay at the church and help out Earl and Charlotte until we returned.

The carriage ride in was enjoyable as was all of the time that I spent with my love, but my attentions were a bit distracted knowing that I may soon be engaged. The route into Charleston was familiar but always new. There were many creatures scurrying about as well as the constant activity along the salt marshes. Herrings, egrets, crabs, dolphins, and mullets were always making their presence known. A welcomed diversion to my one-track mind.

Soon after we arrived in Charleston, we proceeded down East Bay Street to one of the nice inns along the waterfront. It contained a small café that was run by one of the many free people of color in Charleston. That was one of the many peculiarities of the South and Charleston in particular. There were free Africans who had come here as skilled craftsmen or slaves that had bought their own freedom and were living quite lavishly alongside the aristocratic whites. At most levels the free Africans were considered equals. Several hundred of these people of color actually owned slaves themselves. A poignant, ironic commentary of the times. Even the free Africans would betray their better judgment for wealth and power.

Nonetheless, Kelley and I ate a delicious Charleston lunch of crab soup and shrimp with grits. I was particularly fond of the shrimp and grits. It was a delightful stew of shrimp, sausage, and spices served over warm cheese grits. The cuisine in Charleston was a wonderful blend of the Caribbean Islands, the African Mainland, and the Western European pageantry.

It had a little home-grown Southern hospitality thrown in for good measure. The meal was quite fitting of this day.

Following the meal, Kelley and I took the carriage on down East Bay Street around by the Waterfront Park. This area was later known as the Battery. I parked the carriage and we strolled up and down the waterfront, finally stopping to sit on a bench. There was the sight where I proposed.

"Miss Kelley Prose, I kneel here before you and before God to ask for you to be my wife. From this day forward I will vow to honor, protect, and serve you in all ways and in all things. You give me the confidence to excel. You are my motivation and my reward. Please accept this ring and accept my proposal. Will you be my wife?"

Kelley giggled a bit and replied, "Of course I will marry you. We already decided that." She had this way of making a very serious moment more relaxed. "But have you asked my father?"

"He gave me his blessing to ask you. I assume he will give us his support to go through with the wedding," I said.

We sat there and held each other, looking out over the bay toward the old Revolutionary War fort before deciding it was time to head back toward Johns Island. I was much more relaxed on the trip home, having accomplished another goal. My life, like most people's, seems to be made up of a series of challenges or milestones. Each one must be overcome or accomplished. There is a small time of rest before one is off to the next challenge. Life is a lot like a vessel at sea. Having made it over one large wave is cause for celebration, but only a minor celebration before the next wave looms over the bow.

PARTNERS

KELLEY DECIDED THAT WE needed to visit her grandmother who lived on a large plantation adjacent to the seashore. Her name was Eleanor Ledbetter. The family all called her Gram. She was the benefactor to Mr. and Mrs. Prose, supplying them with the land and resources to establish their large plantation on Johns Island.

Gram's land was on one of the barrier islands that was discovered by Admiral Seabrook. Kelley's grandmother was a special lady. She was very wise and kind-hearted to all she met. Kelley's grandfather, Mr. Ledbetter, had died some years back. Currently, Gram had a small group of employees that helped maintain her land. They also farmed the land as sharecroppers. Although I had grown up so close to the seaside, I had not spent much time on the beach. I was looking forward to that as much as meeting Gram.

Kelley and I proceeded down the main road, sometimes referred to as Bohicket Road. Bohicket was the name of one of the tidal creeks that the road crossed over. This was truly one of the most beautiful drives in this area. There was a large canopy of live oak trees lining each side of the road. It appeared as though we were riding in a tunnel, a green tunnel of foliage with every earthy scent surrounding us.

We arrived at Gram's large house around mid-day. It was a lovely house similar to the Prose plantation. It was white and had large Roman columns to support the roof. The front porch was wide and had several tables set up for afternoon or other entertaining. The view from the house was even more magnificent. It looked out over the beach. The constant roar of the surf and waves was loud but somehow provided a calming effect. I could not wait to stroll the beach with Kelley.

We were met at the front door by Gram. She was as nice as everyone had described her, welcoming us in with hugs and kisses. We proceeded to a parlor just inside the main foyer. We sat down to a lovely table set with a fine lunch. We began to eat right away, so our big news for Gram would have to wait.

As we began to eat our dessert and enjoy some coffee, Kelley decided it was time to share the great news. "Gram, Josiah and I are going to marry," Kelley said. She was not one to beat around the bush.

Gram's eyes lit up and she responded, "I am thrilled, my dear! This is the best news a grandmother could hear. I am so glad that your husband will be in a different line of work than running a plantation. You two will be perfect together."

I was not sure what she meant by the comment about the plantation, but I did not want to pursue that discussion at that time. I was more interested in putting on some more comfortable clothes and heading down to the beach for a stroll.

Kelley had told me of her love for the seashore. She spent a lot of time here at her grandmother's while growing up. I was not surprised to see Kelley frolic like a small child out on the sand. It brought out her fun-loving side that I had grown to love and to need. Again she helped me to loosen up. To not be so serious. I needed that in my life. I always felt like I had to carry the weight of the world on my shoulders.

Although I had been to the seashore previously as a small child and had grown up on the marsh, I saw things that day that I had never seen before. We found sand dollars, hermit crabs, and various seashells. Kelley said that some of her fondest childhood memories were of walking on this very beach with her grandmother, finding shells, watching birds, and just talking. I could see how she felt that way. The beach clearly had a calming effect on me. Like a lot of things around this area, it becomes a part of who you are.

I did manage to sneak a kiss or two from Kelley out on the beach. Although my nature yearned for more, I was determined to maintain my high moral responsibility and respect her reputation until marriage. Like so many other things in life, it is easy for a minister to preach about things that he has not been challenged with himself. I wanted to be able to help people without a guilty conscience. I wanted to preach morals to the youth without being a hypocrite.

Kelley and I returned to Gram's house for dinner. Afterward we sat out on the front porch and enjoyed the cool breeze coming off of the sea. I was eager to learn more about Gram. Her life and her views were interesting to me since I felt that Kelley had more in common with her grandmother than with her own parents.

After some small talk about our future plans, I asked Gram, "What did you mean when you said you were glad that Kelley was not marrying a plantation owner? I mean no disrespect by this question, I was somewhat flattered by your response." Kelley and I had already agreed that we would not discuss our views on slavery with others at this time since it could get us in a lot of trouble if word got to the wrong people.

Gram replied, "The plantation owner's life is quite challenging. Storms, drought, and insects make it a difficult way of living. It can be very profitable as you can see by our surroundings here, but it can be trying on a man and his family. In addition, the institution of slavery is drawing to an end. Most people will not say that in public, but I can. I am an old woman; no one puts much credence in what I say. Even though they know I am right." Gram sipped her hot tea and continued, "Slave owners have proven themselves to be immoral and greedy. We here on this plantation tried to always treat our slaves better. But better than what, freedom? You cannot treat someone better than giving them freedom. Freedom to dream, to fail, to love."

"It is interesting that you say those things," I replied. "I have wrestled with some of the same issues myself. Being a pastor, I have to consider what God says about all of these social issues. The Bible says, 'Man cannot serve two masters.' There is one master represented by slavery. It is centered on greed, wealth, and power. The other master is God, represented by love, compassion, and humanity. I agree with you that the question of slavery will have to be answered eventually. I am just not sure what form the answer will take."

I felt a kinship with Kelley's grandmother. She was wise. The wisdom that comes with age and observation. I knew why Kelley looked up to her the way she did. We talked about other things for the rest of the evening before turning in for the night.

The next day Kelley and I had breakfast and then loaded our carriage for the half-day ride back home. I began to cherish the carriage rides with Kelley. It gave us a chance to talk uninterrupted for hours at a time. The beauty of the spring landscape helped set the tone for a relaxing yet deep conversation. Kelley seemed to feed off of some of the comments her grandmother had made the night before.

"Josiah, I think my grandmother is right. Slavery as we know it may not be around 20 years from now, but I do not want to wait that long to help someone I love, namely Miss Pearl. She raised me from an infant. On the plantation, you have a real mother who loves you, but it is your mammy who changes you, bathes you, feeds you, and sings you songs. Miss Pearl has dedicated the last 20 years to me and now I am going to help her," Kelley said with passion.

"What are you proposing we do?" I replied, already knowing she wanted to set Pearl free. "Do you think your father and Guilford would let Pearl go? Would they let you buy her freedom?"

"Josiah, we are going to help her escape! We will come up with a plan to get her up North or out West. Somewhere that she can have her own house and garden and raise her own children," Kelley said matter-of-factly.

"For you, my love, I will do anything, but we must be smart about this. We will not rush into anything. Let's make a plan and we will find the right time to make it happen. The last thing I want to do is to get you mixed up in some of my dealings. That could jeopardize our wedding and even your life," I said.

I dropped Kelley off at the Prose plantation around mid-day. Mrs. Prose, who had a large amount of lacy material in her hand, greeted us at the front door.

"Kelley, dear, come on in. I have selected the fabric for your wedding gown. We need to have it made as soon as possible. We also need to go over the guest lists as well as the location. I was thinking we would have the wedding right here on the front lawn," Mrs. Prose went on as quickly as you please.

We had not planned a wedding date yet. Most likely it would be in the early fall when the temperatures had cooled for an outside ceremony, but that would not stop Mrs. Prose. The old saying "Hell hath no fury like a woman scorned" could be amended to say, "Hell hath no fury like a Southern woman planning a wedding." I bid Kelley farewell and returned to my house and the church.

Earl, Charlotte, and I sat down to catch up on things. They had been busy keeping up the church while I was preoccupied with Kelley. I let them know that Kelley and I wanted to help

Miss Pearl and her husband escape. We did not have any idea as to how we would do it, but we were dead set on making it happen. I gave Earl and Charlotte my standard speech about how they did not have to get involved if they did not want to.

Earl laughed. "We a team. Now Miss Kelley is part of our team. We will get Miss Pearl and her man on to freedom. We needs to take our time and think how to do it. That old hag seems to work well when you need her. Let's just study on this for a while. We will come up with something."

It was clear that God put Earl and Charlotte in my life for a reason. They kept me grounded and focused and motivated me all at the same time. I loved them like my own parents. They were probably more supportive of me than anyone else in my life. I turned in for the night knowing that I was behind on my sermon writing. I planned to spend the next several weeks preparing a sermon series on love and how to treat others. These were the sermons that I had always wanted to give. These were the ones that I had hoped would help change people's hearts and minds. I knew I would have some extra time during the week since Kelley would be tied up with wedding planning.

I devoted myself deeply to Bible study. I wanted to fully understand the principles behind slavery and what God's Word said about it. The beginning of the Bible opens with stories of the Jews being enslaved in Egypt. Moses is the chosen one to help set them free. Later in the Bible, the Egyptians enslave the Israelites again, and again God helps them to be free.

There are other phrases in the Bible that individuals use to support the concept of slavery, but most of the time they are misinterpreting the definition of slavery. Slavery in the Bible is simply the ownership of one human by another. The definition of slavery does not include torture, inhumanity, domination, degradation, or torture. As I previously came to realize, that was the real sin. Slavery in all forms is wrong in my mind. Jesus came to free all people from their bonds.

I could not come right out and say all of these things as I felt them, so I had to tell many of the Biblical stories to show how God always freed His people and how we were instructed to love one another, "another" meaning everyone.

Several weeks later, I had the opportunity to go to Kelley's house for dinner. Her mother wanted to review the wedding plans with me to get my approval. This was a no-win situation. While I preferred a small family ceremony at the church, I was not about to challenge my future mother-in-law on her grand wedding plans. Besides, her heart was in the right place. She did want to do something wonderful for her daughter. If Mrs. Prose ended up looking like the queen socialite of Johns Island, all the better.

The wedding was to take place on the front porch of the Prose plantation. Chairs would be set up in the front lawn to view the ceremony. Flowers would line the aisles. It was to be quite a production. Immediately following the ceremony would be a lovely reception for all of the guests with food, wine, and a cake to follow. Kelley had asked for a small area to be set up on the other side of the slave quarters for a celebration of their own. She wanted the Africans to share in her joyous day.

"I do have one request, Mrs. Prose," I chimed in shyly. "Since I am the only preacher in this area and it is not appropriate for me to marry myself to someone, I would like to ask my grandfather to marry Kelley and me. I believe you have heard me speak of him, Pastor J. K. East."

"Well, of course, Josiah; that would be fine. This is your wedding too you know." Mrs. Prose graciously accommodated my request. I was satisfied, having accomplished this one goal. I did not ask for anything else. I simply graciously agreed to all of the plans that Kelley and her mother had envisioned.

Kelley and I finished the discussion with her mother and then went on a nice stroll around the plantation. We walked down to the pier on the marsh where we sat and caught up on the events of the past few weeks. Other than at church, we had not seen much of each other during the past little while.

"Josiah, have you come up with a plan to get Miss Pearl out of here?" Kelley asked. It was clear she was feeling the excitement of helping others just as I had felt.

"Not yet. Earl and Charlotte and I are all pondering ideas, but we need to be sure it is safe or Miss Pearl and her husband could end up free in heaven instead of free here on earth. I did have an idea though. Perhaps all the events of our wedding day will provide enough of a distraction to help a few Africans disappear. Maybe that old hag or one of her friends will come around that night. They may even want to attend our wedding.

I am sure your mother would love to have such unique guests attend her only daughter's wedding," I said.

"That may work again. We will have to see. Folks haven't seen one of those hags in a while. They may need a little reminder of what she is all about prior to our wedding," Kelley said. "And I will make sure people around here see her a lot."

The next day Kelley came to the church for the day. It was decided that both Kelley and Charlotte would craft some materials to wear that would make them look like that ol' hag. They could both carefully sneak around the island at night to be seen by only a select few. This would start the rumors flying again that the Hag was back and looking for more skins or souls to take. We needed a certain sense of fear to make these plans work.

Charlotte again reaffirmed her position on impersonating a hag. "This is asking for trouble. Dat hag may not like me mimicking her. She real. She gonna come around here one day and let me know what for. I will do what you ask, but I don't like this."

I tried to calm her fears. "Charlotte, you are a good Christian woman. God will protect you from that hag." I am not sure if my words helped.

The beginning of summer came as well as the heat. It was a great time to grow delicious crops but not a fun time to be outside in the middle of the day. Folks were more active at night, which gave Kelley and Charlotte a chance to be seen as the ol' hag. They would hide in the bushes or shadows. Sometimes they would be seen on folks' front porches counting broom bristles or holes in a strainer. I think Kelley enjoyed it greatly. She was a little mischievous by nature. A little naughty. Not in an immoral or devious way, but more playful.

"Scaring folks can be fun," she said. "Especially those folks that are misbehaving at night anyway. Some of them might even be scared straight!"

I took some time in early summer to write my grandfather a letter requesting that he officiate our wedding ceremony. He graciously agreed to wed us and to a few other special requests that I had for him. His presence would make the day even more special than it already was shaping up to be. Both he and my Grandma East were two icons of faith in my life.

Kelley and I picked October 17 as our wedding day. Fall would be far enough along that the weather would be nice and cool. Neither Kelley nor I wanted to sweat the whole way through our ceremony. Nor did we want the aroma of the unbathed to outdo the aroma of sweet flowers on that day.

As August was drawing to an end, we all realized that we would have to finalize our plans to get Miss Pearl and her husband, Jed, away to freedom on our wedding day. We decided to use the Hag again to make it appear as though the couple had been taken away, never to be seen again.

Kelley stepped up her hag activities. She was sneaking out of her house several times a week. Some of the Africans saw her sneak off but they had no idea what she was up to. They would never tell on Kelley for fear of what the punishment might be for meddling in her affairs. Besides, they all really liked Kelley and she liked them at a personal level.

WEDDING

IT WAS TWO DAYS before our wedding arrived, October 15th. Earl, Charlotte, Kelley, and I all met at the church to go over the plan one more time. We had to make sure we all knew where we needed to be and at what time. It would be very difficult to accomplish our goal if any problems arose.

I reviewed the plan. "Just after Kelley and I cut our wedding cake, there will be a lot of toasts and consumption of wine. We will give the wine a few minutes to take effect. It will be much easier to fool everyone if they are impaired by the spirits. The spirit of the wine I mean. That's when Kelley will sneak away from our party and you, Charlotte, will sneak away as well."

They all seemed comfortable with what would happen next so we did not need to review it further. We did say a prayer knowing that was the last time we would all be together alone before the wedding. Starting the next day there would be several parties and family functions to attend. Both Kelley and I had rather large families from all over South Carolina. Most were due to arrive the next day and stay for a week or more. Kelley and I planned our honeymoon trip into downtown Charleston for a few days before returning as husband and wife.

As is customary, we had to practice our wedding the day before at the Prose plantation. Kelley's mother was in charge of showing everyone where to be. She kept saying, "The difference between a dream wedding and a nightmare is poor planning." I actually enjoyed the fact that her mother took control, as it gave Kelley and me the opportunity to sit back and relax. We giggled and looked into each other's eyes. We were really quite smitten with one another. It made us both act rather silly, but it was fun.

We had a lovely party that evening. It was a great chance to reunite with family members that you rarely see. That is the way of the world these days. Families are becoming more and more spread out due to the inventions of boats and trains. It is easier to move and travel.

I also enjoyed the chance to meet Kelley's extended family. They were like my family, a collection of the good, the bad, the crazy, and the wonderful. I think all families are like that. Although it may not be appropriate to say, I think families are like behinds; they may not be pretty, but you are stuck with the one God gave you.

It was difficult to part with Kelley that night. I knew the next time I saw her she would be dressed in her gown. The next time I saw her, I would be moments away from becoming her husband. The one thing that I had wanted most since returning home from Seminary was within my reach. I kissed her goodnight and told her I loved her. I felt a bit nervous.

She, on the other hand, was excited. I could not tell if she was excited about our wedding or the plan to free her beloved Miss Pearl. Either way, I knew tomorrow was going to be an unforgettable day.

I boarded my carriage and began to drive myself back home. As I reached the gates, a few hundred yards away from the Prose house, I saw a small figure running back into the bushes. It made a screeching noise, almost a laugh, and I heard it say, "Be careful, Preacher Man. Be careful messin' with dem hags."

Needless to say this scared me at a level I had never been scared before. I whipped the horses wildly and raced home as fast as two horses had ever been. That was clearly not Kelley and I knew Charlotte was home with Earl preparing food for the wedding feast. This may have been my second encounter with a real hag. Once in the dream and once tonight. Maybe Charlotte was right. Maybe the Hag would seek revenge on those who mock her.

Needless to say, I said several prayers that night and did not sleep very well. On top of my excitement about the wedding, I had to deal with seeing the real Hag. I dare not tell Charlotte for fear that she might get scared and not help us with the plan. I lay in bed and waited for the dawn.

The morning came. Charlotte had made a breakfast fit for a king for Earl and myself. The wedding was not until 4:00 p.m. She knew we would not eat much between now and then with all the preparations. Charlotte had also made me a lovely suit of fine black silk to wear on this special day. She took care of me as her own son. It was nice to feel that love.

Earl had crafted Kelley and me a new carriage for a wedding gift. He was a skilled craftsman with wood. One of the best in the South I would guess. It was a great gift that we would take on our honeymoon and use from that day forward. It had a thick and sturdy wood floor that could carry the weight of four people or more and all of their luggage.

Earl and I reviewed the plan one last time. It was a little peculiar that this time, I played only a small role in helping to set free these slaves. I did, however, inspire others, which I guess was my goal all along. I just had to be sure that no one was hurt or caught in the meantime.

Around midday, my Grandpa J. K. East came over to see me. I wanted to ride with him over to the Prose plantation. I knew he would have a calming effect on my nerves and I just enjoyed his company. As Grandpa approached on his carriage, it was clear that he had received my letter. There was an African young man sitting alongside of him. This was one of my little gifts to Charlotte and Earl for all they had done for me.

I called Earl and Charlotte out on the front lawn of the church and I asked them if they would be able to watch after this slave that had accompanied my grandpa from Horry County. Grandpa did not own slaves, but he had asked one of his parishioners to lend him this one for the trip. They agreed.

"They call him E. J.," I said with tears in my throat. "His real name is Earl Junior."

"Oh thank You, Jesus!" I heard a wail come from Charlotte. "The Lord is wonderful great."

Earl approached me with tears in his eyes. I had never seen Earl cry. "This is the greatest thing anyone ever done for us," he said.

"I only regret that he will be with you for a few short days. We have told everyone that E. J. will be helping out around the church for a few days while my grandfather is in town. You all enjoy this time together. You will be reunited one day forever," I said. With that, grandpa and I boarded my new carriage and left. Earl, Charlotte, and E. J. would follow soon behind in another carriage.

I so enjoyed the carriage ride over to the Prose plantation. My grandpa and I had the chance to reminisce about my youth. How I used to help him in the garden when I would visit his house each summer. He was also one of the wisest men I knew when it came to matters of morality. He always seemed to know what I was thinking even when I was not sure what I was thinking.

"Josiah, I knew you were special even when you were a small boy. I knew you would make a difference in people's lives. I do not know everything you are up to these days, but I am sure you are trying to make this world a better place. Do what is right in God's eyes and everything will be just fine," Grandpa said.

He really did not need to say more. Shortly thereafter, we arrived at Kelley's house. It was odd to call that Kelley's house since soon she would have a new house with me. The Prose house was decked out in glorious splendor. I must say it looked like a storybook picture of what a princess's wedding would be. A Southern princess nonetheless.

Surprisingly, I was not very nervous as the ceremony approached. I guess people aren't nervous when they are absolutely sure that they are doing the right thing. I knew Kelley was the one for me. I was sure that there would be hard times and times when we weren't getting along, but I had faith that it would all work out. I knew that I would want to work it all out with her. She was worth it.

Shortly after our arrival, Earl and Charlotte arrived. I did not formally greet them. It was better that I not act differently than most Southerners would act regarding the help. I did manage to look over to be sure they brought all of the food and other supplies that were needed for all of the evening's activities. Speaking of being confident, I was also confident that our effort to help Miss Pearl and her husband to freedom was also the right thing to do.

It was customary for the bride and groom to not see each other the day of the wedding until the ceremony, so I was secluded in a parlor on the backside of the Prose house. My grandfather was with me. My father did come back to say a few words before taking his seat.

"Son, I am quite proud of what you have accomplished in your life thus far. I know I do not tell you these things often, but I do feel them. Your faith is a model for all of us. Your work ethic is admirable. Your choice in a bride is exemplary. I look forward to watching you and your grandchildren grow. I love you, son," my father said with tears coming down his face. I thanked him for his kind words and he departed to take his seat alongside my mother.

It was a few minutes before the service. After a quick prayer and a hug, Grandpa and I walked out onto the porch to take our places. The scene was magnificent. A layer of leaves blanketed the surroundings of the Prose household. The area around the house was cleared to set the chairs for all of the guests. There were several hundred people in attendance from all over the island as well as family from other areas. The center aisle between the chairs was lined with white flowers, lilies, magnolias, and carnations.

The Africans were able to watch from a distance. I was glad for this because I viewed many of them as family. Those that helped raise me as well as those that I had collaborated with recently. I heard it told that your wedding is the one day in your life when you feel like everyone loves you. I can see that now. I felt like everyone wanted me to be happy and I wanted the same for all of them. During your wedding day, time stands still. The real world is postponed.

Kelley's mother had planned every aspect of the wedding to make it perfect. I was not sure if all this effort was for Kelley or to make Mrs. Prose stand out in the history of Johns Island regency. No matter what the reason, it was set to be a special day and I appreciated her efforts to make Kelley happy.

The band was set up on the porch adjacent to where Kelley and I would stand. The Proses' grand piano was there as well as a violin and flute. They played the sweet soundtrack to my happiness. The music abruptly stopped right at 4:00 and the traditional bridal march began. Kelley appeared from the tent just behind the aisle of chairs.

The world stopped. The radiance of a beautiful woman on her wedding day is unsurpassed even by the sun. I shuddered a bit. This loveliness was to be mine. She loved me. I felt this deeply in my soul. Kelley proceeded down the aisle to me with slow deliberateness. My anticipation was intense.

The ceremony began and seemed to go by too quickly. There was one moment of humor when a spider crawled out of Kelley's bouquet onto her hand. Kelley does not like spiders, but she managed to hold back her scream by simply flicking the spider off. We both knew it was something we would laugh at later, but we wanted to maintain the decorum and reverence of the moment. The ceremony concluded with a kiss. The first of many as husband and wife.

Now for the fun part. Mrs. Prose had set up a large tent-like structure on the lawn of the house. This was the location for the post-wedding festivities. There was a tremendous amount of food of all types as well as wine and of course the wedding cake. Neither Kelley nor I drink wine, but we were glad that all of the guests would be consuming it. It was part of the plan.

The reception following a wedding is a fun event. All of the stress of the actual ceremony has passed and everyone can take off their suit coats and relax. I thoroughly enjoyed it. The Africans had their own post-wedding gathering in a barn on the other side of the house. This was one of Kelley's requests. She wanted the slaves to share in all of her happiness. As darkness fell, we cut our wedding cake and shared it with all of the guests. It was quite nice, a pound cake with a rich buttercream frosting.

After all the guests had eaten their cake and resumed their dancing, Kelley slipped away from the crowd. I remained to mingle with our well-wishers. The plan was beginning to unfold.

After a few moments, Charlotte caught my eye from just outside the tent. She dare not enter for fear of drawing attention to the situation. She motioned for me to come out. She was a little frantic but managed to speak quietly so not to raise suspicion. "Mr. Josiah, it ain't there. It's gone. What am I gonna do?" she panted.

"Slow down, my dear. What's gone? What do you mean?" I replied.

"Dat hag costume that I was to use. It gone. There was one for Miss Kelley and one for me. Mine ain't there," she replied. I knew at this point the plan was ruined. I wondered if someone had found us out.

I had only a moment to think when we all heard loud screams coming from the barn where the slave party was taking place. We all rushed to investigate the commotion. It reminded me a lot of the first time I met Charlotte at the Prose harvest celebration. The circumstances were similar.

As we approached them, we saw all of the Africans running out of the barn except for a few that were too scared to move. There was a dark figure moving through the barn. It was a woman. It was a hag or at least it appeared to be. I rushed over and grabbed the Hag, gently of course, and said there is nothing to fear. I pulled the old cloth hood off of the figure as well as the stringy Spanish Moss. It was Kelley.

The whole wedding party erupted into laughter. While this was an unusual prank for a wedding, it seemed to fit in well knowing Kelley's personality and the amount of wine the guests had consumed. Charlotte and I were laughing along with all of the rest. Although we were in on the surprise, it was still funny. We knew we would have to wait until another day to help Miss Pearl and Jed gain their freedom.

Kelley burst into laughter. "I got you!" she cried out joyously. "I got you, Miss Pearl!" Kelley had a history of playing practical jokes on Miss Pearl. The problem was that Miss Pearl and Jed were not there. They were nowhere in sight.

As the laughter died, a loud, shrieking voice came from down the Prose drive.

"You don't got them, I do. Heeee." The figure said as it disappeared into the woods dragging two people with it. The people appeared to be Miss Pearl and Jed. The Africans all screamed even louder this time. Charlotte screamed, "That's the real Hag. That's her. She don't like being mocked."

A few of the men raced up the drive to look for the bodies that the ol' Hag had grabbed.

There were no signs of anything. No bones, no blood, nothing. I was convinced that this was the real Hag. The same one I dreamed about. The same one that had spoken to me the prior night at that very spot. I was scared. The wedding festivities began to wind down at that point. All of the guests were given a small torch or gas lamp to help navigate their way. They were all truly fearful. I could not blame them, as I was scared too.

Mr. and Mrs. Prose seemed a little shaken as well. Mrs. Prose was clearly scared by the presence of the Hag again around her house.

"Why does she come here? Are we bad people?" Mrs. Prose asked.

Mr. Prose seemed a little more concerned with losing two slaves. The whole event was a bit surreal. We had planned to have Charlotte dress up like the other Hag and lead the Africans away at a safe distance. But Charlotte was with me the whole time.

We did not have to act afraid or confused—we really were. Charlotte may have been right; that hag did not like being mocked. She had come to seek some revenge. While the events of the night had been a bit unnerving, it did make for a memorable wedding day. One of those days we would tell our grandchildren about fifty years down the road.

After everyone had departed, Kelley and I thanked her mother and father and departed for our house back at the church grounds. Her parents had gone a bit overboard with the whole ceremony, but it was lovely and great fun for all involved. We parted with our new carriage full of wedding gifts, which we planned to open the next morning.

As we pulled out of the Prose drive, both of us were quite nervous about what might be lurking in the cool Charleston air. Kelley and I reflected on the joys of the day. The benign conversation was interrupted by Kelley.

"Pull the wagon over in that field for a moment," she said.

I obliged, not knowing her intent.

She leaned over and gave me a passionate kiss. One of those you feel deep down. Needless to say our longing for one another was satisfied right then and there. It was very close to a spiritual experience. To become another person, your wife, the love of your life. That feeling is incredible. The gift of passion and intimacy is one of the most special gifts that we are given.

We finally arrived back home on the church grounds. On top of the deep emotional connection, I also felt a youthful, playful lust. It was quite fun actually. But I did have the urge to ask Kelley a few questions about the way the plan unfolded the night before.

"Who did you find to be the other Hag last night?" I asked. "Charlotte told me that the costume that we hid away for her was missing."

"You are kidding with me, right? I thought you must have found a 'new hag,'" Kelley replied. "I did not see the other costume when I retrieved mine. I assumed you had altered the plan. I just carried on with my part as discussed."

"You don't suppose that was the real Hag again, do you? I hope Miss Pearl and Jed are all right. They may be dead or just gone away," I said.

"We can't do much looking into where they are. That would look a little suspicious. Two newlyweds more concerned with some missing slaves than getting on with their honeymoon. Perhaps Earl and Charlotte can put the word out through the slave network to see what happened and then send word to us in Charleston," Kelley replied.

"That sounds like our only option at this point. Good idea," I concluded.

INHERI-TANCE

We enjoyed a delicious breakfast with Earl, Charlotte, and Earl Junior. It gave me intense pleasure to see them together as a family. All the things that us white folks take for granted, like seeing our kids grow up, takes on a whole new perspective when you see a sight such as this. It also puts the inhumanity in proper perspective as well.

Earl and Charlotte agreed to do a little digging into what had happened with the missing slaves. I made sure they did not dig too deep as to raise suspicion upon themselves or myself.

Kelley and I planned to go to downtown Charleston for our honeymoon trip later that day. We would be staying at her family's lovely home in the heart of the city. Following breakfast, we returned to our house to open the many wedding gifts that were given us the previous evening. Our plan was to open them at the reception, but with all of the uproar over the Hag situation, we did not have a chance.

The gifts were numerous. Again, one of the benefits, or curses, of Kelley's family's wealth was the abundant number of friends they had and the generosity with which they gave gifts. Whether it was true generosity or simply an effort to outdo their Johns Island competitors did not matter. The gifts were quite nice. Some functional, some elegant, and some impractical, but they were all generous and we were thankful nonetheless.

One gift in particular caught our eye; it was an envelope from Kelley's Gram. Kelley opened it with a bit of excitement in her eye. Gram was known for being quite thoughtful and generous with her giving, especially to Kelley, whom she was quite fond of. There was a brief note that Kelley read aloud.

My dear Kelley and Josiah, I am so proud of both of you. You demonstrate a passion for life and love that is so rarely seen in today's society. Always keep your focus on God, each other, and your children. You will have a long and happy life together. I am leaving you both my estate on the beachfront and funds to maintain it as your wedding gift. It will be transferred to you upon my death. Please think of me and your late grandfather as you enjoy it.

P.S. Please beware of that Hag. I hear there have been some wandering around my house.

Kelley began to laugh and cry at the same time. I must say that is one of the unique characteristics that God gave to a woman. The ability to be so happy that you become somber. Men either laugh or cry, never both.

Kelley then screamed out loud, "It was Gram! She must have been the other Hag. How did she know what we were up to? When we get back from our honeymoon, I am going to go see her and find out. My Gram is a clever lady. That's where I get it from."

Kelley and I were a little relieved, having solved the Hag riddle. I was glad that we would not have to focus on that during our honeymoon.

It was a bit overwhelming to think that Kelley and I would have this large plantation on the oceanfront all to ourselves one day. Kelley was raised in that world, but I was not. I did not know what it was like to have all of these nice things. To have nice places to go. It would be an adjustment. But I knew I could not let potential wealth deter me from my life's work of preaching and helping others.

Kelley and I proceeded to pack our belongings in the carriage for the trip into Charleston for our honeymoon. My parents had given us a significant stipend of cash to pay for all of our activities while on our honeymoon. It was a very special gift knowing that my parents are not wealthy and this took a significant amount of their resources.

This trip into Charleston, like all the others I had taken with Kelley, was a pleasure. This was my first trip as her husband and she as my wife. I do not think I quit smiling the whole way. Kelley was beaming as well. We had really connected at a deeper level. The fall weather had brought in a bit of a chill so we were snuggled up close to keep warm.

The first few days of our honeymoon were quite typical of what you would expect newlyweds to do. We strolled around town without a care in the world, we ate at some really nice places, and of course we spent some time alone in our hotel room. All the waiting was worth it, both morally and physically. Kelley and I were satisfied. The relatively pristine world that we were in was insulated from all of the emerging chaos.

These were tumultuous times in the South and in Charleston. It was the day of the Presidential elections. Almost all Southerners agreed that if Abraham Lincoln was elected that that would surely cause eventual secession from the Union. The North was convinced that slavery must end, not because they were an altruistic people that loved Africans, but because they knew it was difficult to compete with free labor. In reality the labor force in the North was not treated much better than a common slave, but they were free. That was a huge difference. Without freedom, one can never strive to achieve more.

The next morning we awoke to a great bustling about town. It was November 7th. A fever had taken hold. The word had come down that indeed Lincoln was elected. The steadfastness of the Southern people was about to reveal itself. It was a strange sight to see many of the Charleston elite, namely judges and other government employees, renouncing their position and affiliation with the federal government.

Kelley and I were both in an awkward situation. We both supported the South. We both supported the right of all states to make laws and govern its people in a way that was sensible. We both, however, realized that the institution of slavery was immoral. It was also evident that slavery would not be able to sustain itself. There were too many pressures pulling it apart. As much as I personally loved the old South and the simple way of life, I could not morally or Biblically support slavery. I did feel that secession was not an unreasonable approach to the potential crisis. I could support the creation of a Confederacy if its goal was the elimination of slavery. Was that even a possibility? I could support a moral and humane Southern country. Only time would tell what course South Carolina would take. I was deeply concerned.

Kelley and I decided to stay around for a few more days in Charleston. It was becoming more and more difficult to relax with all of the fervor. There were nightly public rallies at the courthouse and Institute Hall. It was quite an interesting time. I felt as though we may be witnessing a piece of history. Perhaps the beginning of a Southern revolution or the beginning of the end for Southern ideals.

Kelley and I decided it was best that we return home. We knew word would spread to Johns Island about the unrest in town and I may be needed to quell fears. Although most of Johns Islands residents did not own slaves, our area was dominated by the aristocratic landowners, including Kelley's parents. I never believed that her father was an inherently bad person; most Southerners never knew a different life beyond slavery. I hoped and prayed that all would see the inhumanity in this practice and abandon it rightly. I was prepared; however, the concept of secession would bring out the worst side of all involved.

As Kelley and I were pulling back into the church grounds, we saw her father waiting on us in his carriage. He had a very serious look on his face. With both Kelley's and my history with helping the slaves, we were always concerned when people came around that we were not expecting. That is one of the burdens of our activities; we always have to look over our shoulder.

Mr. Prose greeted us in a somber tone. "Welcome back. I trust you had an enjoyable time. I regret to greet you with bad news, but your Grandma Ledbetter has become ill. She may not make it much longer. You should go to her straight away."

Kelley and I did not even get out of the carriage. We turned around and headed back down Bohicket Road toward the seashore. Needless to say Kelley was sobbing heavily. I tried to console her with one arm and drive the carriage with the other. My hope was that we could arrive at Gram's before she passed away. I knew Kelley would regret not getting to talk to her Gram one last time. I also knew this meant we might not get an explanation for Gram's hag story.

As we pulled up in front of Gram's house, Kelley jumped out and rushed inside. I took a brief moment to secure the carriage with one of the servants. Kelley rushed past several family members into Gram's room and knelt beside her bed. Gram was weak and could barely speak. She was still the grand lady in charge of her surroundings.

"Give me a few moments alone with Josiah and Kelley. I have seen the rest of you for the last several days. Let me visit with them a while," Gram stated with some authority.

She still was the matriarch. Everyone responded to her commands. She had earned that right, not by being a tyrant, but by being loving. The throne built on love is always honored; the throne of intimidation is always destroyed.

Everyone else left the room except for Kelley and me. We knelt down beside her bed and simply listened. We knew that Gram's words of wisdom were limited in time and number. We did not want to waste the moments with our idle thoughts.

"Were you surprised that the ol' Hag visited your wedding?" she said with a bit of a chuckle. "Don't worry, those two are safe far from here. You two have a great mission in your life. Make this world better. Help people. Help those that most need it. This world will one day change. The institutions, the way of life, and you two will be needed even more. Stay strong. Please utilize this house and the wealth I have left you in your mission. I love you both dearly."

With those comments she was gone. Her eyes closed and she drew a final breath. This was a great woman and she was going home to be with her Lord. Kelley and I both sobbed greatly. It was evident that Gram had become a large influence on my life after a few short encounters; I knew Kelley must have really been touched by the lifetime of interactions. When great people touch our lives, the impact goes on forever.

The next day was spent preparing for the funeral. Although Kelley's family was very influential and Gram had numerous friends and acquaintances, the funeral was to be small. This was Gram's request. She had also requested that I perform the service. I was deeply honored.

We laid her body to rest on the property under an old live oak tree. It was a lovely spot adjacent to the shore and the inlet. A more beautiful spot may not have existed anywhere on the island. The service was fairly short, but I tried to sum up my feelings and those of the other hearts touched by her in a few simple Bible verses. Pastors are always faced with a great dilemma when performing funerals—how do you sum up a life of great deeds in a few moments? In addition, how do you capture the small things people do that really change others' lives so greatly? We do our best. If nothing else, perhaps we can stir others to recall their own special memories of the deceased and smile a little. Smile on the inside while pain is on the outside.

Kelley and I stayed at Gram's house one more night. I guess it was our house now, but we both still wanted to call it Gram's house. This place was too special, too revered to be called ours. We had to figure out how best to keep this house and farm running smoothly while at the same time maintaining our house and the church. Luckily, Gram had her farm set up to run itself with the foremen, who were former slaves, overseeing all of the work in the field. They were all paid well and therefore were very loyal and trustworthy. For the time being, we planned to trust the foreman to keep the place in good shape and keep the operation profitable. We would visit as often as we could. Eventually we would have to make some tough decisions about where we would live, but for now, the church was our life.

We set out the next morning for home. Kelley was in a somewhat happy mood. She was reminiscing about her summers with Gram at the seashore. "I often wondered if those walks on the beach with Gram meant as much to her as they meant to me," Kelley said. "I maintain the simple things in life are what make it special. Seeing a special bird or finding a sand dollar are what I most remember. Life is a series of cascading events. Any small interruption, good or bad, can forever change history."

I was amazed at Kelley's depth of thought. She was right.

SECESSION

It was now mid-November. The secession of South Carolina from the Union was being contemplated by many of the elder statesmen and the local folk alike. Abraham Lincoln was preparing to take office the following January and the overall picture of these United States was looking grim.

There were few distractions on the horizon. Thanksgiving was approaching. This was a great holiday around here when we all celebrated the blessings of the Lord with family and friends. It was a tradition that went back to the early settlers in colonial days. We planned to have another picnic at the church to celebrate this season and the fall harvest. I think we all knew deep inside that this might be one of the last peaceful Thanksgivings for a while.

As always, autumn had special meaning to the folks on Johns Island. The crispness in the air gave all a new vigor. A new motivation to get out and do things. The fall crops were coming to harvest. We had our fill of sweet potatoes, greens, broccoli, and pecans. In addition, the tidal creeks teemed with crabs and shrimp as well as a variety of seasonal fishes. We all enjoyed these things with a sense that they may change for all of us soon. No one really knew what the election of Lincoln would come to mean for our state or our area, but we knew what had been foretold. Secession and possibly war. No one wanted to think about that, but we were all preparing to deal with it as necessary.

Kelley and I were looking forward to our first Christmas as husband and wife. The holidays were always a special time to me. It was a time to see family, to renew one's faith, and to celebrate life. This year, we were going to spend the weeks surrounding Christmas in Charleston with Kelley's parents. They had a nice home in Charleston where we had spent our honeymoon. I was really looking forward to being in our beloved city during this time of year. There was so much activity, so much joy. I hoped that would be the case this year.

I was also excited about my opportunity to preach during this season. Kelley and I would plan to return to Johns Island every Saturday and Sunday so I could fulfill my duty to the church. It was more than a duty, it was my love. I was called to be a minister, just as I was called to help those in need. The two are really one in the same.

We arrived in Charleston on December 20th. It was an important day in the city's history. Just a few days earlier, a group of state leaders had attempted to assemble in Columbia to discuss the issue of secession from the Union, but the meeting was abruptly stopped because of an outbreak of smallpox. Perhaps this plague was a sign from above. The secession meeting then reconvened in Charleston on the very day we arrived. Needless to say, the city was overflowing with holiday anticipation and secession furor.

Kelley and I decided to walk about the city to get a feel for what the sentiment was. It was a little frightening. This talk of secession was real. The talk of war was real. There was a frenzy of hatred and malice. We both knew that the boorishness of the North was about to collide with the stubbornness of the South. The outcome would change all of our lives.

As we made our way down Market Street, a loud cheer came from city hall. There was great fanfare, music, and shouts of victory. It had happened. South Carolina had voted to secede. Withdraw from the Union. Withdraw from the United States. A series of events was set into motion. The inertia of this day was self-sustaining.

I was torn as I had always been about the issues of our day. I was a true Southerner. I did not like anyone telling me or my part of the world how to live our lives, but at the same time, it would be difficult for me to support a war whose main goal was to continue slavery. I hoped calmer minds would prevail and South Carolina would be able to mend its differences with the Union peaceably or at least secede peaceably.

Kelley and I returned to the Prose house in Charleston to discuss the day's events with her parents. Kelley's father was close friends with many of the men attending the secession meeting. In fact, we believed that he was in city hall when the vote took place. Kelley and I knew that her father was an ardent supporter of secession, but even he was leery of a war. Most knew in their heart that little good would come of a war between the states. The economic impact alone would be devastating.

Upon Mr. Prose's return to the house, he exclaimed cheerfully, "Today, the great state of South Carolina took the first step to becoming a sovereign nation or perhaps join with other Southern states to form a Confederacy of Southern states. We seek to uphold our Southern culture and values and maintain the long-standing institutions that have sustained our livelihood."

In the South that is a euphemism for slavery. I knew better than to engage Mr. Prose in a debate. As I had known from the day of my epiphany, I would be in the minority in Charleston if I was outspoken against the "long-standing institutions." In addition, it is rarely a good idea to take an opposing position to your father-in-law. My plan was the same as it had always been, to change the hearts and minds of the Southern people to no longer want to own slaves. Along the way, I and my new partner, Kelley, would help those in need to gain their freedom. Even if that meant going against man's law in favor of God's Law.

My vision was for the South and perhaps South Carolina itself to form its own country. At that time, hopefully rational minds would prevail and outlaw slavery. The Southern Confederacy would be a sovereign nation with a paid workforce. I was not opposed to secession, I was not necessarily opposed to a potential war, but I was opposed to the inhumanity of slavery.

The following Saturday, Kelley and I returned to Johns Island to prepare for Sunday services. Being that this was the last Sunday before Christmas, it would also be the Christmas service. I always enjoyed hearing and giving the Christmas sermon. I, like most preachers, told the story of Jesus' birth. It is one of the most simple yet most moving stories in the Bible. Young and old were captivated. It is a true phenomenon that people just act a little different around Christmas. They are a little nicer, a little more thankful. The Truth of that day is undeniable.

Saturday evening, Kelley and I had the opportunity to sit down to dinner with Earl and Charlotte. I was anxious to hear what they knew about recent political events and how the Africans were perceiving these happenings.

Earl said, "Pastor Josiah, now that South Carolina has left the Union, they want to form their own country. What do you think that will mean to all of us?"

Personally, I was more interested in hearing Earl's wisdom and thoughts on the issue so I replied, "What do you think it means, Earl?"

"Well, it seems to me you can look at this a number of ways. I doubt slavery will end anytime soon if South Carolina has its way. I hear tell that the Union ain't gonna let the Southern states break away, so that would mean a war. That war brings on a whole new set of issues. Overall, I think my chances of living to see freedom are slim," Earl concluded.

"Earl and Charlotte, you are both very special to Josiah and me," Kelley responded. "You will be free. You will live free soon. We will give you some land and let you farm it on your own or we will help you run away. You will taste freedom, I promise,"

Kelley said with all of the passion that I had come to love. And we all knew that she was not kidding. It would happen.

Kelley and I returned to Charleston on that Monday. We spent the rest of the holiday through New Year's at the family's home in the city. I must admit I had an enjoyable time. The city of Charleston managed to put aside some of its secessionist fervor to focus on the real meaning of Christmas. I loved that.

With the holidays behind us, Kelley and I were settled back on Johns Island. We still spent a considerable amount of time between our home at the church and the home that Gram had given us on the seashore. They were only about ten miles apart, but it took several hours or longer to get there based on the weather and road conditions. We knew one day we would have to decide where we wanted to live and how we would continue to take care of all of these responsibilities, but for now we managed.

Word came that other states in the South were voting to secede as well. Talk was that the South was to form its own union or confederacy. The tension between the North and the breakaway states was building. We all hoped that peaceful minds would prevail.

As spring entered the South, there were new chores to be done. We repainted the church and added some benches and tables on the lawn area for future gatherings. We also planted a small garden of spring and summer vegetables. There was also a need to replenish many of the church's supplies that had been depleted throughout the winter.

Kelley and I followed closely by Earl and Charlotte headed into Charleston one morning in April. The goal was to purchase what we needed and then head back home just before dinner. The trip there was somewhat uneventful. Charleston was beginning to resemble more of a military fort than a city, but all of the charm and beauty was still evident.

We were unable to take our usual route home, which took us out by the Waterfront Park. This was where I had proposed to Kelley and we had spent a significant amount of time during our honeymoon. Currently that area was controlled by South Carolina militia with cannons aimed at Fort Sumter. The Fort was held by Union troops and controlled much of the ship traffic in the harbor. It was sad to see one of the symbols of Southern charm being used as a military stronghold, but such was the times. I hoped it would all resolve soon and we could resume our somewhat normal lives.

It was already dark as we departed Charleston. Torches lit our way as well as some light from the crescent moon. The still of the cool spring air was interrupted by cannon blasts. Booming volleys of cannon fire coming from the Battery area near the bay. It was clear—life had just changed yet again for all of us. The hostilities had formally begun. We would all have some intensely challenging decisions to make. These were decisions we had all postponed in hopes that the two sides would peacefully reunite or peacefully part.

We pulled our carriages over and said a prayer. I did not know what else to do. We were all in tears. I held tight to Kelley as Earl held tight to Charlotte. What now?

The many roads that had led us all here were haggard. A new chapter was about to begin for myself, Kelley, the Africans, and for the country. Through it all I knew that my ministry, my life, and my mission would all be a great journey. That journey had just begun. My goal in life was a simple one:

Let it not be said that I was a good man or a great man, for that is subjective. That is someone's opinion. Let it be said that Josiah Whitby did right. Right is not up to the whims of society. Right cannot be bent by the whirlwinds. Right is the blue sky when clouds approach. Right is above it all. Right is right always.

For more information about
Eli Alexander
&
Josiah Whitby
please visit:

www.josiahwhitby.com
elialexander@charter.net

For more information about
AMBASSADOR INTERNATIONAL
please visit:

www.ambassador-international.com
@AmbassadorIntl
www.facebook.com/AmbassadorIntl